Gavin couldn't take his eyes off her. She stepped closer and suddenly, they were kissing. A soft but long kiss.

She pulled away. "I have no idea how that happened." Her cheeks were flushed but her eyes were...blazing.

As he was sure his were. He wanted to pull her close and kiss her longer and harder.

Which was ridiculous. He couldn't be attracted to Lily Gold. His administrative assistant. A woman about to give birth. Harlan Mandeville's great defender. "We just got caught up in the moment."

What moment, though? he asked himself. They'd been standing right here in the nursery talking about how she'd be a great mother. There'd been no flirting. In fact, their conversation in the living room had been kind of heavy.

Then again, maybe that was what "the moment" was about. They'd gotten a little too close too fast.

She nodded vigorously. "Yes. The moment."

"We'll just pretend that kiss never happened," he said.

He could try all he wanted, but as he'd already begun to learn, you couldn't pretend something hadn't happened, even if you hid away in a small cabin.

"Never happened," she repeated, her expression unreadable.

He knew that kiss was all he'd think about tonight.

Dear Reader,

When a nine-months-pregnant woman turns up at Gavin Dawson's family dude ranch, demanding to see him, he has no idea why. Until she says her name. He's been avoiding her texts, calls and emails for a week. Lily Gold is the administrative assistant at the Wild Canyon Ranch—which Gavin has just inherited from the late father he never knew, a man who never acknowledged him. Gavin wants nothing to do with the prosperous ranch.

Too bad, cowboy. Lily needs Gavin's signature and approval to keep ranch business going. She loves the Wild Canyon—it's her home, her security and her baby's future. But when she falls hard for the handsome loner, will he choose the family of two who love and need him...or his life on the road?

I hope you enjoy Lily and Gavin's story! I love to hear from readers, so please check out my website at melissasenate.com and feel free to friend me on Facebook.

Warmest regards,

Melissa Senate

her shop to get a glimpse of her through the picture window. Talk about a glutton for punishment.

She let out a low growl. "You are an infuriating man. Stubborn and callous. I don't even know if you have a heart."

"Funny." He kept his voice steady even as memories flooded him, making his head pound. "That's the rationale Amber gave me for why she cheated with your fiancé. My lack of emotions pushed her into his arms. What was his excuse?"

She looked out at the street for nearly a minute, and Alex wondered if she was even going to answer. He followed her gaze to the park across the street, situated in the center of the town. There were kids at the playground and several families walking dogs on the path that circled the perimeter. Magnolia was the perfect place to raise a family.

If a person had the heart to be that kind of a man—the type who married the woman he loved and set out to be a good husband and father. Alex wasn't cut out for a family, but he liked it in the small coastal town just the same.

"I was too committed to my job," she said suddenly and so quietly he almost missed it.

"Ironic since it was your job that introduced him to Amber."

"Yeah." She made a face. "This is what I'm talking about, Alex. A past I don't want to revisit."

"Then stay away from me, Mariella," he advised. "Because I'm not going anywhere."

"Then maybe I will," she said and walked away.

Don't miss
Wedding Season *by Michelle Major,*
available May 2022 wherever
HQN books and ebooks are sold.

HQNBooks.com

SPECIAL EXCERPT FROM

HQN

*Mariella Jacob was one of the world's premier bridal
designers. One viral PR disaster later, she's trying to
get her torpedoed career back on track in small-town
Magnolia, North Carolina. With a second-hand store
and a new business venture helping her friends turn the
Wildflower Inn into a wedding venue, Mariella is
finally putting at least one mistake behind her.
Until that mistake—in the glowering, handsome
form of Alex Ralsten—moves to Magnolia too...*

Read on for a sneak preview of
Wedding Season,
the next book in USA TODAY *bestselling author
Michelle Major's Carolina Girls series!*

"You still don't belong here." Mariella crossed her arms
over her chest, and Alex commanded himself not to notice
her body, perfect as it was.

"That makes two of us, and yet here we are."

"I was here first," she muttered. He'd heard the argument
before, but it didn't sway him.

"You're not running me off, Mariella. I needed a fresh
start, and this is the place I've picked for my home."

"My plan was to leave the past behind me. You are a
physical reminder of so many mistakes I've made."

"I can't say that upsets me too much," he lied. It didn't
make sense, but he hated that he made her so uncomfortable.
Hated even more that sometimes he'd purposely drive by

Heir to the Ranch

MELISSA SENATE

HARLEQUIN
SPECIAL
EDITION

Recycling programs
for this product may
not exist in your area.

ISBN-13: 978-1-335-40846-4

Heir to the Ranch

Copyright © 2022 by Melissa Senate

For questions and comments about the quality of this book,
please contact us at CustomerService@Harlequin.com.

Harlequin Enterprises ULC
22 Adelaide St. West, 41st Floor
Toronto, Ontario M5H 4E3, Canada
www.Harlequin.com

Printed in U.S.A.

Melissa Senate has written many novels for Harlequin and other publishers, including her debut, *See Jane Date*, which was made into a TV movie. She also wrote seven books for Harlequin Special Edition under the pen name Meg Maxwell. Her novels have been published in over twenty-five countries. Melissa lives on the coast of Maine with her teenage son; their rescue shepherd mix, Flash; and a lap cat named Cleo. For more information, please visit her website, melissasenate.com.

Visit the Author Profile page
at Harlequin.com for more titles.

For my mother, with love.

Chapter One

Very pregnant lady here to see you and she looks spittin' mad.

Gavin Dawson read the text from the ranch's front-gate attendant, wondering what this could be about. He'd been on a break from romantic relationships for just over a year now, so *that* wasn't it.

She must be after a different Gavin. Or Dawson. Or Gavin Dawson.

He didn't have time for this. He was fixing a hole in a remote area of fence way out on his cousins' dude ranch, trying not to think about the bombshell that had dropped on his head a week ago. And failing.

Then again, that was why he was here—back home in Bear Ridge, Wyoming, after years away—hiding out in a small cabin at the far end of the Dawson Family Guest Ranch. To think about it. To get his mind around the shocking news, let it sit until he could decide what to do. The branch of the family that owned this ranch—second cousins—had welcomed him with a place to stay, a horse and not too many questions. He appreciated that and them.

"Whoever she is, she must have the wrong guy," he said to Butterscotch, the mare he'd spent hours riding this past week. The horse glanced up from where she'd been grazing by the fence he'd been repairing. He'd figured he might as well pay back his cousins' hospitality by looking for holes and trouble spots. There were always plenty on a ranch. He'd needed to work, good, hard, old-fashioned cowboy chores. It was when he was alone in the cabin, thinking, stewing, that his gut ached.

He grabbed his phone and snapped a quick selfie, then texted: Can you ask her if I'm the guy she's looking for?

It was a two-mile ride back to the main area of the dude ranch where the lodge and guest cabins and cafeteria were. He'd rather stay here, tightening wire and then moving along on Butterscotch.

He glanced at the photo as he sent it. Not a hint of smile. Wary, weary eyes. Hard-set jaw. Not that he'd probably looked any different a week ago; no one would call Gavin Dawson "happy-go-lucky" or "devil-may-care." But a week ago, Gavin would have said nothing could shock him. And then whammo.

I have a direct quote, the gate attendant texted back. You tell him: Hell yes, he is.

Gavin raised an eyebrow and stared at the text. This didn't sound good.

"I don't know, Butterscotch," he said, putting away his tools and slipping a foot into a stirrup. "Guess we're gonna find out."

On my way, he texted back. Two minutes.

He headed out toward the front gate, the cool April breeze feeling good against his face. He lifted his Stetson, letting the wind whip his hair, snap him into attention, then set it back.

As he neared the barn and stables, he waved at some of his relatives who were leading guests on horseback down the bridle path or running a workshop for kids at the petting zoo.

"Who wants to meet our new baby goats?" He could hear Maisey Dawson call out from her perch on a tree stump inside the enclosure in front of the barn.

"Meeee!" at least fifteen children shouted back, hands shooting up in the air.

Gavin had never had much exposure to kids until he'd come back to Bear Ridge. The six siblings who owned this ranch had a lot of little children among them. Between his pint-size relatives and the guests' children, he was practically run over every time he headed from his small cabin to the cafeteria, and the joyful shriekers always made him smile. Gavin liked kids—as long as they were someone else's.

He arrived at the welcome hut. Standing to the side of the ornate wrought iron gate with its huge D was the most pregnant woman Gavin had ever seen. Despite that, she was dressed for business—in a pale blue pantsuit with a floral scarf at her neck and fancy white cowboy boots. Her long swirly blond hair was in a clip past one shoulder.

And yes, she did look spittin' mad. While staring straight at him.

Had he ever seen this woman before? He didn't think so. He'd remember that face—an equal mix of angelic and fierce.

He hopped off the horse, reins in his hand. "I'm—"

"Yeah, I know who you are," she interrupted, hands on her hips. "I'm Lily Gold."

She waited.

Ah. He knew that name. He sighed hard.

The big blue eyes narrowed. "Yeah, that's right. It's me in the flesh."

He'd been avoiding her letters, calls and texts for a week, ever since he got the news from a lawyer that he'd inherited the Wild Canyon, one of the most prosperous cattle ranches in Bear Ridge, upon the death of Harlan Mandeville. Mandeville was Gavin's biological father—the real bastard in the equation—who hadn't acknowledged him his entire life.

Lily Gold had been Harlan's administrative assistant.

All the air in Gavin's lungs had been sucked out by the lawyer's call; the man had tracked him down three hours south in Wyoming where he'd just finished a six-month contract to turn around a failing ranch, his specialty. He'd done his job well and it had been time to go—in three weeks he had to be on the outskirts of Cheyenne for his next assignment. After the call, Gavin had booked a hotel in Cheyenne, thinking the change of scenery from wilderness to city lights would help him come to terms with the news.

It hadn't. He'd realized he needed to be on home

base, someplace familiar. Staying in Bear Ridge would allow him to drive past the Wild Canyon and see if he spontaneously combusted or just felt like hell. If he had no reaction, which was unlikely, maybe he'd even sneak his way on the ranch to check out the place on the downlow. But for the past week he hadn't gone near the ranch.

Enough of a surprise was how he'd felt when he'd arrived in Bear Ridge. Unexpected nostalgia for his hometown, the ranch country he'd grown up in, though he and his mother had lived in a few different rentals close to town, where Annie Dawson had worked as a secretary in dull offices. He hadn't been back since he lost her six years ago. A yearning for family—real family, not fake like Mandeville—had swelled up somehow, and he'd called his cousin Noah about staying at the ranch the Dawsons had rebuilt not too long ago. And here he was.

No closer to knowing what to do with an inheritance he didn't want, let alone all that it called up in him.

Gut-twisting questions. Bitterness on his mother's behalf. And yes, on his own.

The week he'd been here, Gavin had been trying to figure out what to do with the Wild Canyon. Sell it and burn the money? Only in his fantasies. But he didn't want anything to do with it or his father's legacy. Sell it and start his own bigger, better ranch? That sounded good. Except he'd always know the money came from Mandeville.

So he'd done nothing but brood.

And now Mandeville's administrative assistant—very pregnant and shooting daggers at him with her bluebell-colored eyes—had come after him.

"I'm sorry to put you through the trouble of driving out here," he said. "Especially in your…" His eyes dropped to her belly.

She glared at him. "My what? Condition? I'm fine. Know who's not fine? All the people and livestock your silence has been holding up. Paperwork, invoices, checks all sitting unsigned, the new owner not responding to my calls or emails. So you're coming with me, bub." She pointed her finger at him.

"Bub?" He almost smiled. Was she from a 1940s James Cagney movie?

For just a split second, her anger was replaced by sadness, but then it was gone in a flash, the fury back.

She lifted her chin. "My father always said bub. With the finger jab. He picked it up from his father, who probably picked it up from his father."

"Well, I don't know anything about fathers, so…"

She stared at him. "I do know a bit of your family history, Mr. Dawson. I imagine it's not easy to inherit property from the man who wasn't part of your life. But inherit it you did. I'm asking you to take responsibility for the Wild Canyon so that people can get paid, invoices can go in and out, and initiatives and programs finalized."

He might be the owner of the ranch, but he hadn't taken ownership and didn't intend to until he figured out what he was doing with it. "Look, I'm not prepared to—"

"No, you look," she said, hands back on her hips. "Several people are waiting to be officially hired for various positions after being verbally promised jobs. Paperwork for the new sanctuary for rescued animals needs your signature since Harlan died before that was finalized. Six children are supposed to be given free therapeutic horseback riding lessons at the stables this week, but that's held up too. You like making children cry, Dawson? Oh, and let me see what else. Deliveries aren't coming. The veterinarian is pissed. My mom and gram, who run the ranch cafeteria, need their inventory order approved, and the foreman can't do anything without your say-so. You want them to run out of beans for their prizewinning chili? The cowboys will revolt. No one knows if their jobs are secure, including me. Oh, and speaking of the foreman, he's getting yelled at by everyone because of you. Bub."

Oh hell.

"Let me go put Butterscotch away," he said, giving the horse a double pat, "and I'll meet you back here in fifteen minutes." He needed the breather.

"I could go into labor by then," she said, giving her belly that same double pat.

He felt his eyes widen and tried not to stare at her enormous midsection. He held up a finger and darted into the welcome hut to ask the attendant to have someone ride Butterscotch back to the stables.

"You'll get used to me," Lily said as he rejoined her. "I get things done."

She wasn't kidding.

"You're not really gonna go into labor any minute—are you?" he asked.

She smiled. "I could."

He swallowed and trailed behind her to her red pickup.

But she wouldn't, right?

Lily had come after Gavin Dawson herself because most people wouldn't refuse a woman who was nine months pregnant. After he'd ignored all forms of communication from her this past week, she'd done some research on him, this stranger who was her new boss, the new owner of the Wild Canyon, but there wasn't much, so she'd had to go digging deep.

No immediate family. Staying at the popular guest ranch owned by second cousins, six siblings everyone in Bear Ridge knew, including her. That was how she'd found out, through basic gossip in a small town, that Gavin Dawson, "Annie's kid, who'd been away for years," was staying at the Dawson Family Guest Ranch.

He'd been working on ranches since he was a teenager. Traveled across Wyoming as an in-demand ranch consultant. His reputation was impeccable—she'd called and asked, pretending to be looking for references. The most recent place he'd worked at had referred to him as their executive cowboy/wrangler, which had managed to make her smile. The Three Hendersons Ranch, owned by triplet brothers in their fifties, had said he'd turned their operation and them completely around—from the breeding end to the employees to how the brothers dealt with vendors. The ranch was out of the red, morale boosted, and the ranch and the triplets' relationships with one another on solid ground.

Lily had breathed a huge sigh of relief at the information. It meant he had expertise not just with horses and cattle but with the business of horses and cattle—not to mention people—and that had been all she needed to know. Gavin Dawson wouldn't be just some lucky cowboy plucked off one ranch and put in charge of the place she loved more than anything. The Wild Canyon was her everything. Home. Job. Her family worked there. Her future and her baby's future was the Wild Canyon Ranch. Gavin Dawson would know what he was doing, and what he didn't, he'd learn fast.

She'd thanked her lucky stars at what she'd learned about his background, told herself the man just needed a face-to-face explanation of why he was needed at the ranch, then got in her pickup and went to get him.

That had gotten a chuckle and a "that's Lily for ya" from her mom and grandmother, who'd waved as she'd driven away in her red pickup, telling her to call when she arrived and/or at the first sign of a contraction, just so they wouldn't worry. On the drive over to the Dawson Family Guest Ranch, she'd actually been a little nervous that her well-hidden anxiety over her mission would send her into labor, and she'd give birth alone on the side of the road. Everything depended on getting Gavin Dawson to the Wild Canyon.

Now here he was, sitting right next to her in her truck.

Yeah, she got things done. Often at a cost to herself.

"I've got a question for you," she said, sliding a glance at him. Did he have to be so good-looking? His hair was a sexy mess, tousled, dark and thick under his Stetson, and he was at least six-two with serious muscles. Intense green eyes but with a twinkle, which gave her hope that he wouldn't be too difficult to deal with. She liked his shirt, a dark green Henley to match the eyes. And his jeans. And his dark brown work boots.

Her hormones were doing a number on her.

"Shoot. Not literally," he added with a smile and a bit of a drawl like he was Matthew McConaughey.

All week she had literally wanted to shoot him. "Why didn't you jump to claim the multimillion-dollar ranch you inherited?" she asked. Executive cowboy—who probably earned a small fortune as a ranching consultant—or not. "As I said, I know a little about your family history, that Harlan wasn't a part of your life at all. But why would you sit on the inheritance?"

"Well, that's probably the easiest question I've ever been asked besides my name."

She raised an eyebrow. How could it be? Given what she did know.

"Why would I want anything to do with anything of Harlan Mandeville's?" he said, bitterness landing on the name. "He shirked his responsibility to my mother and never acknowledged me as his child."

She did know about that, a little, what Harlan had chosen to share in those final weeks. Her question might have been easy for him to answer, but the answer itself was anything but.

"When my mom told him she was pregnant," he continued, "want to know what he said?"

Actually, Lily knew that too. Harlan had hid his terminal illness from everyone, but when he finally told her how sick he was, that he only had a month to go, he told her about his regrets too. Including how he'd treated Annie Dawson.

"He said he'd had a vasectomy and disconnected the call." He shook his head. "A lie, obviously, since I'm sitting right here. When I think about him, I think about that."

She glanced at him again, noting the bitter edge in his deep voice. "What if I told you that when he knew his time was coming, he'd expressed his regrets about how he'd acted?"

The strong arms crossed over his chest. "I'd say he was afraid he wouldn't be allowed beyond the pearly gates."

"Maybe so," she said. "But he didn't talk about that. I knew Harlan. I'd never quite seen that expression on his face before. Pure unadulterated painful regret."

"Sorry, Lily, but I'm not buying it. I respect people who take care of their regrets when there's time to make it count. When I was four or five and would ask my mother where my father was, she'd tell me I did have a daddy but that he wasn't a good person and we would make our way in life and we'd be fine."

Lily had actually grappled with that when Harlan had told her about the child he'd pretended didn't exist. She'd been floored to learn about the existence of Gavin Dawson, Harlan Mandeville's flesh and blood. Could you be a good person and do that? She'd worked for Harlan for ten years and had only known him as kind and generous. Tough, yes, but always fair.

She'd asked him straight-out while he'd sat in the padded recliner she'd had moved into the stables, his favorite place, a wool blanket around his frail frame. *Did you have a vasectomy before you met Annie Dawson?*

It had taken Harlan a full day to answer that question. *No*, he said. *It was a lie. A lie I've been thinking about a lot these days.*

That he'd left the Wild Canyon to Gavin Dawson, seemingly a total stranger to Harlan Mandeville, shocked everyone but her. The whispers had flown around the ranch, particularly *Who is Dawson to him?*

"Your mother sounded like an amazing woman," she said. "Strong. Independent. I know it had to be hard raising a baby alone."

"As I grew up, I asked her why she hadn't gone after him for child support, insisted on a paternity test and all that. She said he'd just lie and pay off a doctor to make up a phony vasectomy report and that it wasn't worth trying to go after him." He glanced at her. "She worked two jobs—one weekdays, one weekends—to raise me while Harlan Mandeville sat on his throne at the Wild Canyon. I have no doubt he's in hell right now."

She gasped. "Gavin Dawson, you take that back."

"Take it back? The truth?"

She lifted her chin but could feel it wobble. Dammit. She did want to think of Harlan in heaven, that his acknowledgment of his wrongdoing, his regret, meant he'd been accepted in.

"The Harlan who ended that call with your mother and the man I knew don't line up," she said. "At all, Gavin. Harlan was so considerate of people, a great boss to me and the ranch employees, and very generous."

Gavin let out a bitter laugh. "Tell that to my mother worrying over bills. Tell that to the kid who grew up fatherless and with nothing when he had a rich daddy who pretended he didn't exist. Think about how that might make a kid feel."

She knew it had to be painful. She could imagine Gavin at five, at ten, at fifteen wondering about Harlan Mandeville, worrying that he wasn't enough for his own father to want him in his life. She couldn't reconcile the man who'd turned his back on Gavin and his mother with the Harlan Mandeville who'd been so good to her and her family. A man who'd agreed to fund her idea for a sanctuary for old and rescued animals. For the free therapeutic horseback riding lessons. He'd paid for a ranch hand's father's dental surgery. Instead of firing a cowboy who'd needed bailing out of jail, he'd asked Lily to research a program for him to get his life back on track and promised him a job if he stuck with it. The guy had.

"I just know he deeply regretted his actions where you're concerned," Lily said, turning onto the road that would lead to the ranch. "Lack of actions, I should say. He left you the Wild Canyon, after all."

He frowned. "I don't want to talk about Harlan Mandeville."

As he turned to glare out the side window, she figured she'd leave him to his thoughts. He was 100 percent right about his feelings about Harlan;

of course he was. She had no business trying to tell him Harlan was a good man when that made no sense to Gavin. How could it?

The important thing was getting the ranch in full operating mode.

As they reached the double bronze gates to the Wild Canyon, she waved ahead at Kyle in their own version of the welcome hut, and the gates swung open.

"How long have you been working here?" Gavin asked.

"Ten years."

She felt his gaze on her.

"Ten years? You look all of twenty-five."

"I'm twenty-eight. I lost my dad to a car accident when I was eighteen, and my parents had always struggled financially, so I needed to get a decent-paying full-time job to help my mom. I saw an ad for an assistant to the administrative assistant at the Wild Canyon. And a few years later, when Harlan's admin retired, I was promoted into that role."

"So you have your own assistant too?" he asked.

"Nah. I don't need one. I'm super organized, which is half the job. Harlan added the assistant salary to my new salary, since he figured I'd be doing the work of two people." Another example of his generosity.

Gavin seemed to be registering that but didn't say anything. He was now looking around. The drive up to the ranch house where the offices were was breathtaking and would ensnare even the biggest city slicker with its wild beauty. Land and sky was all you saw for a quarter mile, then the ornate stables, which Harlan had gone all out on. He'd wanted to be able to see the stables from his office and the master bedroom.

The house came into view, a sprawling luxury log mansion. She still couldn't believe she lived here—in an attached two-bedroom apartment in the same luxe post-and-beam style as the house. When she told Harlan that she was pregnant and that the father had disappeared on her a while back, he'd offered her the place. The apartment had always been reserved for the foreman, but he now had four little kids and had moved off the property. Lily's commute to work had gone from a twenty-minute drive with her mother and grand-mother to a two-minute walk. Harlan had offered to add bedrooms for her family, but her mom and gram liked their small house in town, walking dis-tance to the coffee shop and library. Suddenly she wondered if Gavin would start charging her rent. Or ask her to move.

She pulled up in front of the house and put the truck in Park with a satisfying click. She'd done it. She'd brought the new owner back with her. Now she just had to keep the conversation on the ranch, on what she—it—needed from him, and all should go well.

No more talk about his father.

She opened up her door, and Gavin was out and around the side of the truck to hold it for her before she could blink. A gentleman—that should work in her favor too. "The ranch is more than—"

"I've done my research," he said. "I know the basics of the operation. Acreage. Head of cattle. Horses. Number of employees."

Also promising. Unless he was planning on selling the Wild Canyon, which would put her in a panic and leave many of the employees off-kilter.

She wiggled her way out of the truck, no easy feat for a couple of months now. He kind of held out his hands toward her, instinctively, she knew, to catch her if she wobbled.

Yes, a gentleman. Cared about others. This all might go better than she expected. In fact, it gave her an idea. A little pushy on her part, but the right thing for the ranch and maybe even Gavin Dawson. She'd excuse herself for a moment once they were inside and make a pleading call to Harlan's attorney.

"The thing most folks here want to know is if their jobs are secure," she said, glancing at him, then looking out toward the pastures. Sometimes eye contact was needed and sometimes you had to give someone a little space. "Including me," she went on. "Everyone's nervous that the new owner is gonna want to bring in his own people or not know their histories and personal relationships with Harlan."

The strong arms crossed over his chest. "How nice that he had so many personal relationships with everyone but his own child." He let out a breath and hung his head back.

Lily felt that anxious clenching of her chest as she had a flash of her child asking her where his daddy was. She'd had seven and a half months, ever since she found out she was pregnant, to come up with an answer that didn't break her heart, but she hadn't hit it on yet.

When I was four or five and would ask my mother where my father was, she'd tell me I did have a daddy but that he wasn't a good person and we would make our way in life and we'd be fine.

Lily didn't even know if her baby's father was a decent person. She'd gotten sweet-talked by a good-looking guy she'd met at a rodeo corn dog stand, and she'd fallen for everything he'd said, which he'd likely said to different women every weekend. She was a smart, capable person, never been anyone's fool, and she let herself get taken by a man who'd really just wanted one thing: a girl-friend for the weekend while he was in town to see the rodeo with a zillion other people. He had a very common name, and trying to track him down had gotten her nowhere, even with her excellent internet skills. At night, when she'd lie in bed and couldn't sleep, she'd imagine finally finding him.

Oh hi, I'm that woman you ghosted after our whirlwind weekend—I thought we had something special but... Anyhoo, I'm pregnant and...

She could imagine his blank stare, then how he'd bolt.

"What am I going to tell my child?" she whispered, blinking away the tears threatening to fall. As she realized she'd actually said that aloud, she could feel her face flush.

His expression softened, his gaze going straight to her left hand. To the empty third finger. "I was curious about the lack of ring."

"I got ghosted after a whirlwind weekend."

He tilted his head. "So the guy doesn't even know he's about to be a father?"

She shook her head. "Couldn't find him. I tried. And I'll have nothing for my son to go on. It's not like he can post an ad on Craigslist. 'Eighteen years ago, you were waiting for a corn dog at the Bear Ridge Rodeo when a blonde wearing a white tank top managed to squirt mustard on herself. You bought her a rodeo T-shirt to change into and you spent the whole day together, then the night. Same the next day and night. Then you disappeared, no note, nothing. Like she didn't matter, like none of it meant anything.'" She shook her head. "I hate when I'm an idiot."

"Don't be hard on yourself about that," he said. "I doubt there's a person alive who hasn't been blindsided."

"You?" she asked, suddenly very curious. Did he have a girlfriend? A serious one?

"So bad that a year ago I swore off romantic relationships. Still going strong on that one."

"Don't you get lonely?" she asked. "I do, and I have a wonderful best friend and a mother and grandmother, who call or text me every twenty minutes. My phone should ping any second now."

He looked out into the distance. "I like my work. It's enough."

She brightened at that. "The work you'll do here is basically the same. Except you don't have to actually turn this place around. It's thriving. You just have to manage it. Keep it humming and growing."

"We'll see," he said.

She didn't like the sound of that.

She felt her shoulders slump and tried to inject her usual take-charge, can-do attitude, but it was nowhere to be found right now. "For someone who loves order and control, everything about my life is up in the air. Including the most important thing of all—being this baby's mother. I'll bet your mother would have great advice for me."

Ugh, why was she being so…honest with this man? Talking his ear off about her personal life. He was her new boss, first of all. And second, he might seem like a gentleman who opened car doors and rushed to catch pregnant ladies, but who knew what he was going to do. Gavin Dawson's decisions about the ranch would affect her and her family.

"She probably would," he said. "But you know what, Lily? I'm thirty years old. I'm fine. Everything a kid needs to know and feel to go to bed feeling happy and safe, I knew and felt. Yes, I had questions about my father. But I was raised by a strong, smart, independent mother who loved me, took care of me and instilled her values in me. You'll raise your son the same way. The woman who got me to come here with her is a woman who can do anything."

He reached for her hand and gave it something of a squeeze.

Huh. She actually felt better. Lifted up a bit. "You're different than I thought you'd be," she said. "Nicer, for one, given how you ignored me for a week."

He smiled. "When is the baby due?"

"Two weeks to the day." Her left hand went instinctively to her belly.

"Got a name picked out?" he asked, surprising her again.

"Micah. After my father. Now, there was the dad of all dads."

"Well, you'll just follow his example," he said with a firm nod. "What he did as a dad you'll do as a mom. Then Micah Gold gets the best of both worlds."

That was a kind thing to say. She hadn't been expecting this—the kindness.

Combined with his face and long, muscular body, that kindness would have her talking too much. She had to watch herself around a guy like this.

"Well, let me show you your office," she said, heading up the wide steps to the porch.

She could feel him trailing her, his presence overwhelming even outside.

We're going to be all right, she said silently to her son, whom she'd be meeting in just fourteen days, give or take a few. For her baby, her home, her future, for the employees counting on the new owner not making any changes except welcome ones, she'd do whatever she could to convince Gavin not to sell—and especially not to some stranger or corporation. He had a family connection to the Wild Canyon whether he saw it that way or not. A history, a past he could finally dig into. He could make peace with the memory of Harlan Mandeville, which he clearly needed. It would be win-win for everyone.

If only Gavin Dawson would see it her way.

Chapter Two

Gavin looked up at the house, which was even grander and more gorgeous than the photos he'd seen online. A mansion cabin if there was such a thing, polished and rustic at the same time with a wraparound porch. He glanced behind him at the matching ornate stables visible down the pasture. In the immediate area, you wouldn't know this was a working ranch, but when he turned to the left, he could see cattle on ridges, the start of the elaborate fencing and several ranch hands at work. A huge red barn was just visible.

This was his? He'd consulted on everything from multimillion-dollar operations to small spreads with just fifty head of cattle, but the feeling was always the same: he'd felt at home.

Here, though, he just felt…off-balance. The land, the fences, the stables, the pastures, the barn he could see in the distance. All very familiar. But a chill was running up and down his spine because of whose place this had been.

"As you know, since you did your research," Lily said, "the Wild Canyon is huge. The house is relatively private. Around the left side there's an entrance to the office, where the reception desk is—that's where I sit. Your office is just beyond it. The office is open-door 8:00 a.m. till 6:00 p.m. Monday through Friday and closed from one to two for my lunch break. But I'm always on call."

At nine months pregnant?

"When are you starting your maternity leave?" he asked.

"I'm not sure I can take leave," she said. "More than a couple days, anyway. Things are really up in the air."

Gut punch. "Sorry about that."

She moved her hand to the porch railing as if to hold herself up.

He stepped toward her, a hand reaching toward her back. Awkwardly. "Do you need to sit down?"

"I'm fine, but yes," she said. "Let's head inside

the office and I'll show you around and we can sit and talk about the urgent matters."

Dammit. It was why he was here, but everything about this—owning this place, being here, making decisions for the Wild Canyon—felt like someone else's life.

He followed her down the long porch to a doorway with a big sign that read Wild Canyon Ranch Office. Steps led down to the side yard and a stone path with a wooden directional post reading Office with an arrow. There were several Adirondack chairs scattered on both sides of the door, a huge potted cactus at the far end of the porch.

On the door was a whiteboard that noted Lily would be gone until at least two o'clock. It was now one thirty, so she'd gotten him here faster than she'd expected. Scrawled notes were jotted on the board. Inside the office was more polished wood, posts and beams, burnished leather furnishings, reminding him of the lodge at the Dawson Family Guest Ranch. A huge wood desk was in the center. Photos lined the back of the desk, and orderly piles sat beside a computer. Lily Gold, Administrative Assistant was etched across a gold nameplate facing three guest chairs.

"This is my desk, obviously," she said. "Your office is right there," she added, pointing to the right. "Why don't you head in and look around and I'll join you in a minute."

He stared at the door, which was ajar. Harlan Mandeville's office.

People and animals are counting on you, he reminded himself. Go deal.

Harlan Mandeville's office was gigantic. Polished wood and marble, stone fireplace, oil paintings and watercolors and drawings of the Wyoming countryside, the ranch, cattle and horses. A huge ornate desk faced the sliding glass doors with a throne-like padded chair. The office was very clean, orderly. He moved over to the windows, staring out at nothing in particular.

"This is your office now," came Lily's voice. He turned to find her in the doorway. "Harlan always said the chair was so comfortable he could sleep in it."

Oh did he, Gavin thought, trying to keep the snarl off his face.

"Just so you know, Harlan had an open-office policy. So employees, vendors, lost folks—they come through all day long with questions and issues and this and that. If your door is closed, I'll know you don't want to be disturbed."

Closed? Like I'd trap myself in here with all this bad energy? "Well, why don't we get started on the sign-offs so you can sit and relax."

She nodded. "Let me just go get my stack and iPad. I have to make a quick call, so give me five more minutes."

Don't leave me here, he thought as she closed the door behind her.

A chill ran up his neck. His legs felt like lead, so he just looked out the sliding glass doors at the grass, sky and land that always brought him peace. But peace, here, was unlikely.

He had a flash of memory of himself at thirteen, going through the typical teenage angst, riding his bike to the Wild Canyon, which was twenty miles from his apartment, planning to demand to see Harlan Mandeville and be acknowledged. But he got to the gates and all the bluster had gone out of him. If his father hadn't called his mother about seeing his child, getting to know him in those thirteen years, it was because he didn't want to. Gavin had fought off tears, a wall erecting inside him, and he'd thrown a rock at the gates and then pedaled away hard, taking a turn too fast and ending up in a ditch, a huge scrape on his forearm and both knees. The scar on his arm was still there. Always a reminder of who and what his father was—a bastard. That night he'd vowed to strike it rich on his own, have an even bigger ranch than Mandeville, but all his hard work had led him to helping others make their ranch dreams come true. An old girlfriend had accused him of not wanting anything permanent in his life, including a ranch, let alone love or a family or even a dog.

He'd realized she was right. His work kept him from putting down roots. A traveling executive cowboy couldn't have a dog.

A year and a half ago, he'd met someone who'd stirred something in him, made him start thinking about committing to a person instead of to a business contract. She'd worked on the ranch where he'd been consulting on a four-month contract. But like he'd told Lily, he'd been blindsided; the woman had also been sleeping with the married owner of the ranch. The wall in his chest had been reinforced with concrete.

Gavin walked over to the sliding glass doors, which looked out onto the pastures and stables. This part of the porch was around the corner from where the office entrance was. He stepped out and breathed in the fresh, clean April air, trying to just take in the land instead of focusing on all the other stuff. Like his father.

As if he could separate the two—the ranch from the rancher—when he was in Harlan Mandeville's office. He headed back inside, glancing around. A huge oil painting was over the stone fireplace. Bison in the wild. There were no photos on the mantel or the credenza. Nothing personal. The huge desk was tidy, probably Lily's doing. There was a large inbox and it was empty.

He sat down in the leather chair and so far, his stomach wasn't churning. The lack of personal details helped. But then his eyes landed on a small framed photograph. Harlan Mandeville about twenty years ago. Gavin knew because he'd seen Mandeville in town exactly twice as a kid, and the first time he'd looked just like the man in the photograph.

A lot like himself now. Mandeville had been forty when Gavin was born. His mother, twenty-two.

Of course.

Gavin had spotted Mandeville going into the Italian restaurant with a very pretty young woman in a red dress. He'd been ten at the time, which meant Mandeville had been fifty. Gavin had almost rushed up to the redhead to warn her. *He'll dump you in two weeks, and when you call and say you're having a baby, you'll get lied to and a click in your ear.*

But he'd just stood there, his heart pounding.

Gavin grimaced and knocked the photo onto its face, then stood up. He was getting the hell out of here.

But then a knock came on the door.

Perfect timing for Lily to be back. They could take the paperwork outside, he'd sign whatever and then head back to his cabin at the Dawson Family Guest Ranch, where he'd stew and brood some more, coming to absolutely no conclusions. Of that he had no doubt.

"Come on in," he called, anticipating seeing Lily's pretty face and that professional blue pant-suit with the white cowboy boots. Somehow she'd become familiar among all this strangeness, even though she was part of it.

But Lily wasn't alone. She stood beside a man in his forties wearing a suit, bolo tie and cowboy boots. He carried a leather portfolio. "Gavin Dawson, meet Lamont Jones, attorney at law. Harlan Mandeville's attorney, specifically."

Gavin narrowed his eyes at Lily, then at the lawyer. Just happened to be in the neighborhood? What the hell was going on here?

Lamont Jones patted his portfolio. "I have the document to officially transfer ownership of the Wild Canyon to you, Mr. Dawson."

Whoa. A big whoa. "I'm not ready to sign any-thing about taking ownership of the ranch," he said, shifting his gaze from the lawyer to Lily and back again.

"Oh," Lily said, her cheeks flushing again. "I'm sorry, Gavin, Lamont." She turned toward Gavin.

"I thought you intended to do that since you're here to sign off on various paperwork to get the ranch moving again."

Oh hell. Why did he think his signature would mean a thing on paperwork for programs and cafeteria orders if he didn't actually own the ranch yet?

"Look," Gavin said, holding up his hands. "I'm—" He paused, sure he heard the sound of crying. A child crying.

Lily and the lawyer both turned around. Lily stepped to the doorway and peered out.

"Oh, Lily, there you are," a woman's voice said. "I'm so sorry to bother you." A brunette in her fifties and a little red-haired girl, crying and swiping under her eyes, appeared just beyond Lily.

"No, that's okay, Emily," Lily said. "Hi, Acadia," she added, kneeling down in front of the girl. "I'm so sorry you're upset." She slightly turned to look at Gavin. "Emily is one of the cooks in the cafeteria. And this is her granddaughter, Acadia."

Acadia continued to cry, her eyes on the floor.

"We just came from the stables," Emily said. "Acadia was supposed to start horseback riding lessons today, but the cowgirl instructor can't allow her to join the group because that particular new program wasn't signed off on, apparently.

I was just hoping maybe you'd gotten in touch with the new owner?"

Punch right to the stomach. Left hook. Right hook.

The girl couldn't be more than eight years old. She was trying to stop crying; Gavin could see it in her face. Her grandmother had an arm around her.

"Acadia loves horses so much," Emily continued. "She just has a real bond with them. She lost her parents almost a year ago now, and her counselor thinks a therapeutic riding program would be a big help. And the fact that it's free for employees makes it possible."

You like making children cry, Dawson?

No, he didn't.

Lily bit her lip and looked a bit flustered. Right then he knew that although she'd called in the lawyer, she hadn't set this up—the crying girl and her grandmother. He wasn't even sure how he knew that with certainty, but he did.

Gavin knelt down in front of Acadia, who swiped under her big brown eyes and kept her gaze on the floor. "I'm very sorry to hear about your loss, Acadia. Very sorry. I lost my mom and I know how that feels. I'm the new owner of Wild Canyon Ranch, and you can join the horse program today on my say-so. Lily will arrange it with the instructor."

The girl looked up at him, her entire face brightening. "Really?"

"Really," he said.

The grandmother smiled.

Lily smiled.

The lawyer smiled.

The girl smiled.

Who wasn't smiling? Gavin. He was too aware of the chills racing up his spine.

"I'll text ahead," Lily told the woman. "You and Acadia go join the group. I'll also text one of our hands to meet you out front with a golf cart to bring you back out to the stables."

There were thank-yous and goodbyes and excited chatter from Acadia as they headed out.

"Well," the lawyer said, sitting down. "I have some documents for you to sign, Mr. Dawson."

It took a lot for Gavin to hold back his long, tired sigh. He glanced at Lily, who didn't look triumphant in the slightest. Not that he knew her at all, but she seemed a bit subdued.

Because she knows this is hard for you. And for some reason, she cares.

He gave himself a mental slap on the side of the head. *Don't assume anything*, he reminded himself. That angelic face and fierce attitude got you here. Who knows what she's capable of?

Like making him face things he wasn't ready to face. Never would be, probably.

"Once you've read through the paperwork, if you'll sign here and here," the lawyer said with two taps of his fancy pen, which he slid over along with the document. He then placed a thick sheaf of papers on the desk. "Here are the financials. The ranch does quite well."

Gavin read the three pages that would transfer ownership. Harlan Mandeville had left him everything. Complete ownership of the Wild Canyon. He flipped through the financials, noting the numbers. The ranch did better than quite well. It made a mint.

He picked up the pen, his gut beginning to twist. All he had to do was sign his name "here and here" and he was the owner of his father's ranch.

He stared at the line, the pen heavy in his hand. *You like making children cry, Dawson? The veterinarian is pissed. The foreman's getting yelled at by everyone because of you. I'm asking you take responsibility so that people can get paid...*

A stream of crying kids coming into the office—his office—flashed through his mind.

Crud.

He signed. One of the hardest things he'd ever done.

* * *

"Well, I'm not surprised to hear it one bit," Lily's grandmother said, holding up her hand, palm out, for a high five. "My Lily accomplishes whatever she sets her mind to."

Lily slapped her one. She, her mother and grandmother were sitting at a table in the otherwise empty cafeteria, plates of today's special, a grilled-chicken sandwich with Gram's tangy buttermilk mayo and delicious sweet potato fries, in front of them. It was two thirty, just past the lunch hours of twelve to two. Usually the kitchen staff ate before they were swarmed by hungry cowboys and cowgirls, but when Lily had texted a thumbs-up after she'd gotten back to the house with Gavin Dawson, her mom had asked if Lily could sneak away for a late lunch to celebrate the great news.

Great news it was. The ownership was transferred. Gavin Dawson was in. He'd sat at his desk and signed off on at least thirty documents and many more PDF contracts on the computer.

She'd offered to show him around, but he'd said "maybe later" and that he needed to just stare out at the wilderness for a bit, let it all sink in. She'd given him Harlan's keys, which were labeled, went back to her desk and texted so many people who'd been waiting on the new owner that her thumbs got numb. Then she left a note on her desk and the whiteboard on the door that she was in the caf having a late lunch with her mom and gram.

She dipped a fry in the squirt of ketchup on her plate. Lately she'd been craving sweet potato fries. And no one made better fries than her gram.

"So what's he like?" her mother asked, taking a bite of her sandwich. Tamara Gold had offered to come with her to confront Gavin, but Lily had figured her belly would do the trick and it had. Between "her condition" and everything he'd been holding up, she'd had no doubt she'd get him back to the ranch.

People tended to underestimate the three generations of women because they were petite and "sweet looking" with their light blond hair and blue eyes. Lily's fifty-five-year-old mother had a thing for pastel floral clothing, and seventy-five-year-old Gram always had a hand-knit cardigan with one button done up at her neck. But they were fiery, independent women who'd raised Lily to be that way. If someone crossed them or someone they loved, look out.

"He's not what I expected, that's for sure," Lily said. "Not that I know what I expected. Someone slicker, maybe. Arrogant. He actually seems like a really nice person."

"Really?" her grandmother asked with one eyebrow up. Betsy Parker, her mother's mother, always told it like she saw it. "After ignoring your calls and emails for a whole week?"

"Well, I better understand why now," Lily said. "He might be a little bitter about Harlan not acknowledging him his whole life." More like a lot bitter.

Her grandmother pointed a french fry at Lily. "Just like I said when you first told us about him inheriting the ranch. Of course he's bitter. His father knew he had a child out there and pretended he didn't exist."

It wasn't like Lily could say, *But maybe he really did have a vasectomy.* Harlan had told her that was a lie. "Does that sound like Harlan to you?" she asked, looking between the two women. "It's so hard for me to reconcile it with the man I knew."

"Honestly, I can see it," her mother said. "Harlan was clearly a commitmentphobe. Never married but lots of short-term girlfriends. In the ten years you worked for him, Lil, how many girlfriends would you say he had?"

"I couldn't begin to count," Lily said, taking another bite of her sandwich. Some girlfriends lasted days, some a month, but never longer. Harlan always said his love was the land and the ranch, just like that seventies song about the sailor and the sea.

"He never talked about his past, right?" her mom asked. "Before he started the Wild Canyon, his childhood, that stuff?"

Lily shook her head. "I always asked, but he said 'the past was the past and I live in the present.' I don't even know where he grew up. He'd never answer even that directly."

"Well, in the end, he left his son everything," Gram said. "He wanted to make amends."

"But can you?" Lily asked. "Can you make amends when you turned your back on your child from the very beginning? I get why Gavin is bitter."

She tried to imagine tracking down her baby's father only to be told he couldn't be the father and the call disconnecting. Lily hadn't dated for months before the rodeo, which she'd gone to alone to distract herself from her lack of a love life. Her last relationship had ended badly, and she'd decided to stay single for a while, take a pottery-throwing class, learn Italian, go hiking in the beautiful Wyoming mountains. She'd ended up pregnant—and on her own just like she'd been.

"Bitterness is the devil," her grandmother said. "Just eats away at your heart and stomach and soul. Hopefully he'll find some peace with all this."

Lily was going to help him. Yes, partly to protect her and her family's interests, her baby's future. Her job, her home. She loved the Wild Canyon. If he sold it, who knew what the future would hold? But mostly because the man she'd gotten to know today was a good person, kind, thoughtful and clearly compassionate, given how he'd responded to little Acadia. He didn't have to think well of Harlan Mandeville, of course, or anything at all; he just needed to find that peace her grandmother was talking about and look at owning the Wild Canyon as a part of his history.

"He looks a little like Harlan," her mom said, swiping a fry in the tangy mayo. "Not in coloring but they're both very handsome."

That was for sure. After Harlan had told her about Gavin and that he was leaving the ranch to his son, Lily had googled him. He had a great website for his consulting business, with a photo of him on a horse that she'd thought about a lot over the past week. At first, she'd marveled at how good-looking he was, intelligent green eyes, dark hair peeking out from under the dark brown Stetson. But as the week had worn on, she'd see that picture in her mind and mentally throw water balloons at him.

She thought about how he'd immediately comforted the crying little girl in his office. Now she was back to ogling the thought of his face. How he'd rushed to open her truck's door.

Lily was going to help him. She just had to keep her hormones out of it.

Chapter Three

Gavin hadn't stuck around the Wild Canyon once Lily had left his office. Tour? No thanks. Of the property or the house. He'd needed to get away and let the shock of the day wear off. So he'd arranged for a ride share and headed back to the Dawson Family Guest Ranch.

He'd parked by the gate and had planned to walk the two miles to the cabin since he did his best thinking on foot. But he found himself with unexpected and welcome company when he ran into his cousin Rex and his year-old daughter, Chloe, fast asleep in her orange stroller after a trip to the petting zoo.

Gavin had already told his cousins about the inheritance, and every one of them and their spouses had said the same thing: accept ownership of the ranch and see how it goes. They'd acknowledged that there was a lot to process but that processing was probably the best thing that could happen to him. His cousin Noah reminded him that the six siblings had inherited their own ranch as a broken-down, dilapidated mess from their late father, a raging alcoholic and neglectful parent, and none of them had wanted anything to do with the place at first. Now the guest ranch was thriving, a very popular vacation spot, and it had brought the Dawson siblings, who'd been scattered across the state, back together. So of course they were pro take-the-opportunity.

He quickly filled in Rex on what was going on now, how being at the Wild Canyon had made him feel. "But you know exactly what I mean," Gavin added. "Couldn't have been easy for you and your siblings. Coming back home and dealing with all that."

"It wasn't. But we've all told you it was worth it. And it was. Being back here, dealing with our past, changed us all in ways you wouldn't believe. I used to live on the road, like you. Now I live for my family." His gaze shot to little Chloe, her long dark lashes against her cheek.

Family. There was that word again. His mother had been gone six years and she'd had few relatives, so it had been just him for a while now. Maybe that was why he'd had such an unexpected reaction when he arrived at the dude ranch. These people were his family, even if they'd barely known each other growing up.

But Harlan Mandeville wasn't family. He was just DNA to Gavin. DNA meant you were blood related, but that clearly didn't make you family. To some people.

Chloe started to stir, and Rex's expression changed to what Gavin would call happy anticipation. It was very evident that he loved this little girl. Chloe had become his daughter when he married her mother, Maisey, who ran the day care and children's programs at the ranch. Gavin knew Rex wasn't exaggerating about living on the road; he'd been a US marshal and now worked alongside his brother Ford as a police officer at the Bear Ridge PD. Rex gave him a cousinly pat on the shoulder and continued down the path toward the lodge with Chloe.

Gavin had never thought much about getting married; it hadn't really occurred to him that he would until he met the cheating liar, Lana, a year and a half ago. At first, the idea of committing to someone, caring about someone to that degree, had been so foreign and he realized he must have been pushing women away all these years. But she'd broken through—then took that sledgehammer to everything he'd been feeling.

Lily Gold flashed into his mind. Nine months pregnant. Ghosted by her child's father before she could even tell him she was expecting. He had never just walked out on a woman he'd been involved with and couldn't imagine doing that.

Especially to Lily, who was so…hard to stop thinking about. He wondered what she was doing, if she was feeling okay. He didn't know a thing about pregnancy or what it was like in the final month, but it couldn't be all that comfortable. Maybe he'd stop off in town and bring her something for all she'd had to put up with—her calls and texts going ignored all week and the stress that must have caused her. Driving out to the dude ranch, when she probably should have been close to home, to confront him and bring him back, which she certainly had. Getting the lawyer over with the paperwork in record time. She'd accomplished quite a lot.

He tipped his hat—literally—to her.

Yes, he'd bring her something. He had no idea what. But something. Which meant he was going back to the Wild Canyon.

He had to, he supposed. It was his now and

he had to come to terms with it, and he certainly couldn't do that from this small cabin at the dude ranch.

He went inside the cabin and packed his stuff into his two duffels, took the suit bag off the back of the bedroom door, then gave the place a basic cleanup and headed out. He texted Rex that he was going to the Wild Canyon for the time being and to let the others know along with a thanks for inviting him to stay as long as he needed.

Rex texted back a smiley face in a cowboy hat and a thumbs-up.

A half hour later, he was in the gift shop in town, asking the saleswoman what a nine-months-pregnant woman might like.

She beamed at him. "My specialty, since my daughter is due next month and I'm the grandma-to-be expert."

Two minutes later, he had the hardcover book *Comfort and Wisdom for the New Mother* and a long, buckwheat-hull-filled body pillow that the saleswoman said helped her daughter sleep more comfortably and that she carried with her everywhere she went, even to the coffee shop. Lily had been wearing blue today, so he assumed she liked the color and chose the one the saleswoman had called periwinkle. She'd tied a ribbon around the pillow and did some sort of magic with scissors to make it all frilly, then did the same with the book and handed him his big bag.

Well. First he'd taken ownership of his father's ranch and now he was bringing a lady gifts.

He drove back to the Wild Canyon, the route both familiar and not at the same time. He constantly felt like he should be making a turn, that he couldn't possibly be on his way to his father's ranch. But he was because it was his now. That was going to take a while to get used to.

Gavin stopped at the gate and introduced himself to the young man inside. The guy straightened up and shook his hand and seemed a little flustered at meeting the new owner, so Gavin tried to set him at ease. Then he got back in his truck and headed up to the house, keeping his eyes off the stables that Harlan Mandeville loved so much. He wasn't interested in anything the man had cared about.

He pulled up in front of the office, Lily's pickup there, which he was glad to see. Any sign of her was a comfort, ironic after avoiding all signs of her for the past week. He grabbed his bag and got out, movement in the high grass adjacent to the porch and leading to the woods catching his attention.

He could see a furry body and then two black ears, one floppy, one upright. And then heard a whimper. An injured dog? He set down his bag. "Hey there," he called out, walking over.

A snout poked out of the grass. A border collie mix, slightly wagging his tail. No collar.

The screen door opened and Lily stood there, the setting sun lighting up her blond hair. "You're back," she said.

"Know this guy?" he asked, pointing at the dog, who was half in the grass, clearly timid.

Lily came down the porch steps and studied the pooch. "I've never seen him before. He must smell the sweet potato fries I brought back from the cafeteria earlier. Poor guy. He's skinny and so dirty. I'd kneel down to say hi but those days are over for a few weeks at least."

He got down on one knee. "Come here, buddy. We're friendly." The dog slowly inched over and sniffed Gavin's hand. "I heard him whimper, but he doesn't appear injured, at least outwardly. Maybe he's just hungry and scared."

Lily nodded. "A couple of our hands who bunk on the property have dogs and so I always keep a jar of doggy biscuits, and I think I might even have a bag of kibble from the last time I pet sat for one of them." She made her way up the steps—slowly—and into the office, then came back out with two biscuits and handed them to him. "I do have some kibble, but I can't lug the bag down myself."

"I'll get it," he said. "Here you go," he added to the pooch, holding out the treat.

The dog gobbled them both up.

"He's a beautiful dog," Lily said.

"He is," Gavin agreed. "I guess I could take him in for the night and then I'll call the area shelters and see if anyone's looking for a missing dog. I can have him checked out for a microchip from the vet in town."

She smiled. "And to think for a week I thought you were horrible—for ignoring me, I mean."

He stood and picked up the big bag from the gift shop. "Well, I was horrible for ignoring you, Lily. I should have at least acknowledged that I got your emails and calls. No matter how shocked I was about the inheritance and how I was feeling about it. No excuse."

She tilted her head. "Apology accepted."

"Let's get this guy inside and fed. He definitely needs a bath too."

"You hear that, cutie?" she asked the dog. "The new owner likes dogs and it's your lucky day."

They headed inside, the dog slowly following.

His father's ranch. Gifts for the admin. For Lily. And now a dog.

What the hell was his life coming to?

* * *

"The bag of kibble's in that cabinet," Lily said, pointing. "There are two bowls beside it. No bed or toys, unfortunately."

He gave the dog a scratch behind an ear. "I'm sure this guy is just happy to get some food and attention."

The dog looked up at him with his soulful brown eyes. Aw.

She eased down into her chair, which had two cushions on it. She could use a third. But right now she was more focused on what a surprise Gavin Dawson was than on her tired feet—even in her very comfortable white cowboy boots—and her sore muscles.

"Feeling all right?" he asked, concern in those green eyes. "Now that I'm here—for the time being, anyway—feel free to start your maternity leave immediately. There's no need for you to be working, Lily, or going up and down those steps. I know how ranches work, and there are always a million things going on—you don't need that on you."

Oh my word. Her mom and grandmother were going to fall over themselves at how thoughtful her new boss was. Harlan had been kind, but she wouldn't have called him thoughtful. It hadn't often occurred to Harlan to think about others, but when a need was pointed out to him, usually by Lily on behalf of an employee, he always said yes. "I would have trained a new admin, but when it would have been time to do that last month, Harlan confessed he was terminally ill. So of course I stayed put to guide the ranch unless Harlan absolutely had to be consulted or sign stuff."

"There is a lot to sign," he said with a smile.

Oh that smile. She hadn't seen much of it, but it lit up his entire face.

"And since you clearly won't work me too hard," she added, "I'll stick around to ease you into the Wild Canyon."

"If you're sure," he said. "Anytime you need to leave, you just take off, okay?"

She grinned. "Twist my arm."

He got the kibble and the bowls, the dog sniffing the air. "I guess I'll call you Buddy—very unoriginal—until we know if you belong to anyone," he said to the dog, setting the food bowl by the cabinet. He went into the restroom and filled up the other bowl with water, then set it beside the food. The dog ate and lapped up the water, then padded over to Gavin and leaned against him.

"Oh, you're in trouble if he's a real stray and no one claims him," Lily said. "That dog has chosen you."

Gavin's eyes widened. "I can't have a dog. I don't have a home."

"No?" she asked with a laugh. "You have a mansion. And thousands of acres of land."

He frowned, then understanding dawned. "I guess I do have a house and some property."

She eyed the huge bag he'd carried in from Bear Ridge Gifts Emporium. "So what's in the bag?"

"My way of apologizing for making you charge after me," he said.

Her mouth almost fell open. Had he gotten her a present? "You didn't have to get me anything. It's my way to charge after people."

He laughed, and she realized it was the first time she'd heard it. "Well, here." He brought the bag over to her and set it on the floor in front of her chair. "One of the gifts is heavy and one is light." He reached in and pulled out a long pillow with a multicolored ribbon around it.

She gasped and slowly leaned forward. "A body pillow—I need that! The one I have is so beaten down. I love it—thank you." Omigosh. She ran her hand along its soft cover, admiring the pretty blue color. She glanced down at her pants. Had he chosen blue because she was wearing blue and assumed she liked it? Based on what she knew of the guy so far, she wouldn't doubt it.

Be still, my heart.

He smiled and put it back in the bag. "And this," he said, handing her a small hardcover book, also with a ribbon around it.

The man knew how to buy a pregnant woman gifts. *Comfort and Wisdom for the New Mother*, she read, looking at the cover, which had an illustration of a silhouetted woman holding a baby. "Gavin, this was really thoughtful. I'll start reading tonight and keep it on my bedside table. Thank you. You shouldn't have but I'm glad you did. I love presents," she added, hugging the book to her.

He smiled again, and she was glad she was so big and ungainly and couldn't launch herself at him for a hug. How many more times was he going to surprise her today?

She realized she was staring at him and set the book down on her desk. "So…we can give Buddy his bath in my yard. I have a hose right there. I'll just zip in to my apartment to change and to get soap and a towel." Just when she needed a change of subject, when she was so touched that she might cry, a dog had managed to come along out of the blue. "Not that I can really zip anywhere nowadays."

He smiled, his gaze dropping down to the floral scarf at her neck. "Sounds good."

She pushed up out the chair, Gavin reaching out a hand to pull her up. "Thanks, I needed that." To keep herself from staring at his face, Lily looked at the dog. "Come on, Buddy. Time for your bath." Soon she'd be saying that about her own baby. She couldn't wait to give her newborn son his first bath and smell that baby-shampoo scent.

She pushed open the screen door and locked up the office since it was now past six, and they headed down the long porch and turned right, where her private entrance was. "I can enter through the main house too, but I never do."

"Have you lived here long?" he asked as she got out her key.

She shook her head. "About six months. When I told Harlan I was pregnant and that the baby's father was nowhere to be found, he offered me the apartment, rent-free." She was about to add something about how generous it was of him but caught herself. Gavin didn't need that kind of thing rubbed in his face. And Harlan's generosity to her was evident in what she'd said.

He nodded. "I'll honor that," he said. "The arrangement for your home."

Relief flooded through her. "I appreciate that," she said, then opened the door, so aware of Gavin behind her, in her home, her sanctuary. She loved this apartment. The entry opened into a good-sized living room with sliding glass doors that led to a private deck and field. There was a beautiful stone fireplace, which she'd stared into plenty over the winter, wondering what it would be like when the baby came. Soon she'd know.

"Very nice," he said, looking around.

"You can take Buddy out into the yard. It's even fenced in. Harlan thought I'd need privacy once the baby came."

Again, he didn't respond. He opened the sliding glass doors and let Buddy out, then followed him. She watched him look around and could imagine all that was going on in his head. To suddenly be thrust into this new life, new home, new people. New dog, even. And deal with the family history the inheritance brought to the forefront.

She dashed into her bedroom and took off her pantsuit and the scarf and changed into her very favorite maternity yoga pants, which were a silvery white, and a long, stretchy baby blue V-neck T-shirt. Ahhh. She unclipped her hair and left it loose, pushing it behind her shoulders.

She went into the bathroom, which was getting smaller these days and harder to turn around in, and grabbed her oatmeal bodywash, which would be okay for Buddy, and a towel. They'd just use a little soap to get the grime off.

She went outside to find Gavin in exactly the same spot, standing at the deck railing and looking out at the field, his new friend right beside him.

She wanted to grab her phone from her pocket and snap a photo, but that would be weird.

Why was she having so many feelings for this man? She knew why, of course; she was immersed in his private business—literally—and he was so damned attractive. And nice. He'd bought her a body pillow. And a sweet book on motherhood.

He'd rescued a dog.

She'd better be very careful where those feelings took her because her hormones were raging and she was particularly vulnerable nowadays and Gavin Dawson was her new boss. Who could upend her entire life by selling the ranch. And even if he didn't sell the place, he might just bring in someone to run it for him. Management—and who knew what that might look like. It could be perfectly fine—or really bad. She'd likely lose her apartment and all the built-in perks that made the job she was perfect for so perfect for her.

In any case, she'd better not let herself get too attached to the man because she couldn't count on his staying.

Something she knew about all too well.

An hour later, Buddy was sparkling clean and fast asleep on a fleece blanket at the edge of the rug by the fireplace. Gavin sat beside Lily on her sofa, herbal tea for her, coffee for him and a plate of homemade—by her grandmother—chocolate chip cookies. She had her legs up on the coffee table, her feet bare, her toenails painted a metallic blue. She looked a lot more comfortable in her long T-shirt and yoga pants than she had in her professional pantsuit.

"You don't have to dress for work," he said. "Just be comfortable."

"Harlan told me the same thing, but seriously, I like my work clothes. My mother and grandmother surprised me with two maternity pantsuits, so you'll be seeing the blue one and my peach one a lot the next couple of weeks. And I have a bunch of stretchy dresses. Add a cardigan and a little scarf and I'm ready for the office."

"I guess Harlan does sound like he was a good boss," he grudgingly said. No dress code because she was pregnant. Giving her the apartment attached to the house. Adding an assistant's salary to her own since she'd be doing two jobs in one. Agreeing to free programs that cost a small fortune. Not many ranchers he knew would have said yes to an animal sanctuary for old or injured horses and goats. A pair of ancient llamas were due to arrive in a few days. All this meant big vet bills. But apparently that had been fine with Harlan Mandeville.

It bristled. He found it hard to accept. Jerks were

jerks. No gray area there. And a man who turned his back on his own kid, who left a twenty-two-year-old woman alone and pregnant and having to get a second job as a weekend waitress to support her child, was a jerk.

Of course, it was entirely possible to be good at business, which included how you treated your employees, and a bastard in your personal life. Gavin had met many of those types. Harlan Mandeville was clearly in that category. And when it came to his father, Gavin liked categorizing.

"You said your mother and grandmother work in the cafeteria?" he asked.

Her face lit up at the mention of them. "They run the place and have a few employees to help with prep and cooking and cleanup. They love that kitchen. It's open for lunch and dinner for all ranch employees and highly subsidized. They serve the usual cowboy fare—chili and corn bread, burgers and meat loaf. Harlan kept the prices low—grilled cheese and soup for two fifty, a burger for three bucks, with fries. All fruit and vegetables are a dollar to encourage eating them."

"I guess when a ranch is making so much money, the owner can afford to support programs that retain good employees." There. The flip side of Harlan Mandeville's supposed generosity: good business practices. It was the kind of viewpoint he'd often recommended to his clients. Offering subsidized grilled cheese and allowing his admin to wear workout clothes while pregnant didn't make Harlan a great person. Just a great businessman.

"Did Harlan leave you anything—in the will?" he blurted out. He'd been wondering but hadn't meant to just ask.

"Nope. You inherited everything."

"I'm surprised to hear that," he said. "He could have set you up to be comfortable."

She shook her head. "I'm his admin, not his daughter. As I said, he paid me very well. Harlan wasn't a big spender. Everything he made always went back into the ranch. The furnishings are nice and the horses are treated like gold. But except for his fancy belt buckle that he wore to rancher-association meetings and decent cowboy boots, he didn't throw money around. He was very practical."

A cheapskate was more like it. "Maybe that's why none of his girlfriends ever lasted," he said. "Why he never got married. He didn't want to share his money."

She narrowed her eyes at him, then her face softened. "Actually, you might be right. I was just talking to my mom and grandmother about his many girlfriends and how he never had a relationship longer than a month. Maybe it's because they weren't being wined and dined like they expected. Maybe they left him, not the other way around." She seemed to be thinking about that. "Huh."

Yeah, poor Harlan. Dumped by girlfriends half his age for not buying them jewelry and whatever else. Boo-hoo. "Well, it's not like I understood the man either." Understatement of the decade. Though when he'd been particularly upset as a teenager, or frustrated by his past as an adult, he'd look for the easy answer in understanding Harlan Mandeville. He was a snake. That would appease Gavin until the questions started clawing at him again.

She reached out and gave his hand a squeeze, her skin so soft. Then she picked up her tea and took a long sip, wrapping her hands around the mug. "I'm so curious about Harlan's family. Did your mom know anything about them?"

Harlan's family. He'd wondered over the years, particularly as a kid. Did he have aunts and uncles on his father's side? Grandparents who'd spoil him the way his best friend Cam's grandparents spoiled him with cookies and hugs and toys? His maternal grandparents had been gone by the time he was done with preschool and he didn't even remember them. He wished he could. His mother had said they were wonderful.

"She never mentioned anything about his relatives," Gavin said. "I doubt she met anyone in his family. But she rarely talked about him. I once asked her if his parents or siblings knew about me, but she said she wasn't even sure if he had family. I got the feeling he didn't grow up in Bear Ridge. Mandeville isn't a common name and there are no Mandevilles in town. Or the county. I checked a couple times when I was growing up." He drank the rest of his coffee. "I'm surprised you don't know about his relatives. Sounds like you and Harlan were very close."

"Ish," she said. "Close-ish. He was a private person, always kept to himself. I asked him about his family a few times and he always avoided answering, changed the subject. I'm so close with my family that it's hard to imagine any other way. I don't know what I'd do without my mom and grandmother. Plus, I have some cousins in the neighboring towns."

"Cousins I have," he said. "I'm lucky in that regard."

She smiled and finished the last of her Lemon Zinger tea, then took a bite of a cookie. "My gram makes the best cookies." She finished it, a satisfied ah on her pretty face. "Want a tour of the apartment? It's not so big but it's nice, and I'm almost done with the nursery."

He did want to see more of her home, and he had no idea why. Maybe to determine if she needed anything besides a body pillow. He wanted her to be comfortable. He wanted Lily Gold to have everything she needed—and wanted.

Though if she was getting a salary and a half, she likely earned a decent amount. He hadn't gone over the employee records earlier.

"Sure," he said, standing up and reaching out his hand to help her up.

"I definitely need that," she said, slipping her soft hand into his.

He gently pulled her up, and she landed so close to him. Kissing distance.

She rubbed at her back with both hands. "Usually takes me a good minute to get off the couch, so I extra appreciate the hand."

A surge of protectiveness came over him and he found himself too aware of everything about her. Her pretty face and sweet blue eyes, the long swirly blond hair loose past her shoulders. She might be nine months pregnant but she was so… alluring. And she smelled so good, a scent he couldn't put his finger on. Something floral.

She showed him her bedroom, which had a beachy quality to it, soothing blues and off-whites and a huge watercolor of seashells. "And this is the nursery," she said, pushing open the door just down the hall. "I come in here a lot, just to look around and soak it in. Sometimes I can't quite believe there will be a real, live baby in here in just two weeks and I get kind of petrified. And other times, I'm like 'get here already—be early, baby.'" She laughed and stepped farther inside.

The room was blue and white, like her bedroom. The name Micah was stenciled on the crib railing, the silhouette of a cowboy on horseback beside it. There was a big round rug, a padded rocking chair, a bookcase with a few books in it and a dresser with a long pad atop it. Changing station, he figured.

"I have no doubt you'll be a great mother," he said.

She looked up at him, and he could see that she was touched. "You think so?"

He nodded and reached for her hand and gave it a squeeze but didn't want to let go. So he didn't.

And neither did she.

He couldn't take his eyes off her. She stepped closer and suddenly, they were kissing. A soft but long kiss.

She pulled away. "I have no idea how that happened." Her cheeks were flushed but her eyes were…blazing.

As he was sure his were. He wanted to pull her close and kiss her longer and harder.

Which he couldn't do. He couldn't be attracted to Lily Gold. His administrative assistant. A woman about to give birth. Harlan Mandeville's great defender. "We just got caught up in the moment."

What moment, though? he asked himself. They'd been standing right here in the nursery talking about how she'd be a great mother. There'd been no flirting. In fact, their conversation in the living room had been kind of heavy.

Then again, maybe that was what "the moment" was about. They'd gotten a little too close too fast.

She nodded vigorously. "Yes. The moment. Well," she said. "Tomorrow's a busy day with the two goats coming to the sanctuary at seven thirty, so I'd better hit the ole hay." She smiled awkwardly at him. "I'll walk you out."

She hurried out of the nursery and to the front door. "Thank you again for the gifts. And for carting them in here. I can't wait to use my pillow and start reading my new book."

He'd made her nervous, the last thing he wanted.

"We'll just pretend that kiss never happened," he said.

He could try all he wanted, but as he'd already begun to learn, you couldn't pretend something hadn't happened, even if you hid away in a small cabin.

"Never happened," she repeated, her expression unreadable.

He knew that kiss was all he'd think about tonight. He glanced over at Buddy, who was still curled up on his fleece blanket by the stone fireplace, eyeing them.

"Ready to go, Buddy?" he asked. Truth be told, he could use the company. Company that didn't talk or have lips he wanted to kiss.

Buddy shot up and wagged his tail.

"See you tomorrow," he said to Lily.

But he wasn't ready to leave her.

Chapter Four

At seven the next morning, Lily and Jonah, one of the ranch hands who'd be working at the animal sanctuary, stood looking at the new goats in their pen. The new very old goats. Both at least fifteen, they'd been found wandering. None of the nearby ranchers claimed ownership, so the big animal vet had taken them in but couldn't keep them. One conversation later, Lily had gotten the idea for the animal sanctuary at the Wild Canyon. They certainly had the room. Harlan had agreed to the whole project, and last month, the new barn had gone up a mile out from the main house, pastures created and pens set up. The Wild Canyon Animal

Sanctuary was carved into a huge wood sign that hung on the barn—a surprise gift from Harlan just two weeks before he'd passed away.

She kept turning around to see if Gavin was around, but he hadn't made an appearance yet. Ranches started early, but he knew that. For all she knew, he was in his office, getting a head start on his work.

She wondered how he'd slept last night. If he'd slept. His first night in the house. She'd been tempted to text him to ask but thought better of it when their kiss flashed into her mind. For the millionth time.

She couldn't kiss Gavin. She couldn't fall for him. For many reasons but the biggie being that he'd break her heart in two seconds flat. She had no idea if he was staying for good or planning to turn management of the ranch to someone else or if he'd sell the Wild Canyon.

She was about to become someone's mother, and nothing was going to interfere in her joy over that. Her baby boy deserved a mother who was focused on him. She'd gotten Gavin here, and now she'd turn her attention to being a mother. On getting ready for the big day, which was fast approaching. Thirteen days. Give or take.

Of course, hugging the body pillow to her all night had been a constant reminder of Gavin Dawson. How it had felt to be pressed up against him. Kissing him…

"I think the sign is slightly crooked," Jonah said, squinting up at it in the bright morning sunshine.

Jonah was definitely a glass-half-empty kind of guy. She always tried to get him to see the other side, the half-full side, the mostly not-crooked side of life, but he ran more to pessimism than optimism. Still, he was one of the first cowboys to volunteer to split his usual work with sanctuary chores. Lanky with a mop of dark hair and dark brown eyes and barely twenty years old, Jonah was hoping to own a ranch someday. He was a little grumbly but a hard worker and Harlan had adored him. He'd always said he saw himself in Jonah.

"It might be a tiny bit off," she conceded now that she looked closely. "I'll put one of the maintenance staff on it." She smiled up at the sign. "I wish Harlan were here to greet the first residents of the sanctuary." *You did a lot of good in your life, Harlan, no matter what your demons were.*

The goats had been the first to arrive. Two llamas were coming the day after tomorrow and four horses next week.

Jonah didn't respond. He'd been down in the dumps since they'd lost Harlan almost ten days ago now. Harlan had liked Jonah so much that he'd offered him an "internship" to shadow him, see how a ranch was run, and Jonah had jumped at the chance. The past few months, he'd spent an hour before and after his workday to learn all sides of the business. She'd talk to Gavin later today about whether he'd like to continue that. She had a feeling he might like to learn the Wild Canyon himself before he had a shadow.

"Saw lights on in the main house last night," Jonah said with a grimace.

Lily nodded. "The new owner's here. Which is why the goats are here. Everything's been squared away."

"Total jerk, right?" Jonah asked.

"Actually no. I mean, I thought he might be since he didn't respond to my calls or emails, as you know. But he seems like a really good person. He rescued a dog last night."

Jonah frowned. "Well, I'm sure he'll show his true colors eventually. How soon before he sells the Wild Canyon to some giant corporation in Los Angeles and there are suits running this place?"

"He's Harlan's son," she reminded Jonah. "There's a very good chance he won't sell the Wild Canyon." There was a good chance he would, though. That could go either way.

In his final week, Harlan himself had told Jonah all about Gavin and the inheritance. Jonah had been extra grumpy after that, and Lily had figured he was feeling protective of his mentor, whom he was about to lose. Gavin was an unknown and Jonah didn't like change.

"That's just about bloodlines," Jonah said. "Such bull. We're the ones who were by Harlan's side when he was dying. We're the ones who cried over having to say goodbye. Then this whoever walks in and inherits everything? Just because of unsafe sex thirty years ago? Please."

Lily was surprised she could hold her gasp. "You know as well as I do how complicated and private Harlan was. If he left everything to Gavin Dawson, then that's what he wanted to do. He clearly wanted to make up for the last thirty years, Jonah."

"Whatever," he said, kicking at the post of the fence, which he'd helped build.

Jonah was grieving and upset, and it would take him longer than ten days to feel okay about Harlan being gone. He was young and completely on his own and probably scared that the new owner would send him packing—literally—from the cabin he shared on the property with another cowboy. Yes, she'd talk to Gavin about Jonah, share a bit of his story, and she was sure Gavin would make him feel better about his place here.

"Well, the new old goats sure are sweet," she said, looking at them as they slowly walked around the pen. Breakfast was coming their way any minute, and soon they'd feel right at home.

As hopefully her new boss would.

She had to help that along. Show him around, introduce him to the employees who made the Wild Canyon so special. Like their stable manager, Glory Johnson, who'd slept in an ill mare's stall last night to comfort her. The foreman, David Rodriguez, who'd handled the pressure of the past week with such grace, trying to assure everyone without false hope. The two cowgirls who'd spent hours the other day searching for a herding dog who'd gone missing and then finding him injured, rushing him to the vet. There were such good people at the ranch. Gavin needed to meet them all, get to know them the way she did.

And Jonah, of course. The twenty-year-old and the new boss had a lot in common. They just might do each other a lot of good.

Her heart soaring, Lily watched one of the goats jump onto the log. "Look at that, Jonah!" she said. "Felix is at home already!" The brown goat looked quite happy, while his buddy, Dodie, peered at the log.

"Well, he shouldn't get too comfortable," Jonah said on a frown. "We'll probably all be out of a job in days, and Felix and Dodie will have to find some other sanctuary to live out their days in."

Oh, Jonah. The negativity was fear at work. "Why don't you go meet Gavin yourself," she said. "You might feel more optimistic about the future when you do."

Jonah shrugged. "Maybe I will."

Gavin had surprised her all day yesterday, start to finish. She had to keep the faith, even if she had no idea what Gavin Dawson was going to do with the Wild Canyon.

Gavin had to admit—he liked the log mansion. He'd thought he'd toss and turn all night, sleeping in the master bedroom, but in fact, he'd had a great night's sleep, his new border collie friend snoozing away on the fleece blanket. It was no wonder that Harlan loved the view of the stables, which Gavin could see from the king-size bed, the moonlight shining on the beautiful structure. And instead of that unexpected kiss keeping him awake, he'd drifted off thinking of Lily's blue eyes.

He'd gone to the office at seven thirty, but Lily hadn't been at her desk. She'd made coffee and left a sticky note with a smiley face that said it was fresh and there were bagels and cream cheese— a welcome greeting to him from her mom and grandmother—on the credenza. He'd taken his mug of coffee and bagel onto the porch, just able to see some activity in the distance to the left and some cattle on the ridge. Buddy scampered around the grass, and Gavin made a mental note to call the local animal shelters and the veterinarian's office.

He'd spent the morning meeting as many of the ranch employees as he could, shaking hands and being honest about his intentions—that he had no idea what those intentions were at this point. He'd also met Lily's mother and grandmother, Tamara and Betsy, as he was passing by the cafeteria on his way back to the office. He'd thanked them for the delicious breakfast. Both women were warm and friendly, the family resemblance very strong.

Once he left the cafeteria, he'd looked up the number for the county shelter and called to ask if anyone was looking for a black-and-white border collie mix. No one was. According to the shelter, if Gavin put found-dog posters in town and online and no one claimed Buddy after five days, he could keep him. Or he could always bring him to the shelter and they'd try to find him a new family. He'd then called the vet in Bear Ridge, and they'd said the same thing and that Gavin could bring in the dog to be scanned for a microchip anytime today. He'd do that later this afternoon.

He was almost to the office, anticipating seeing Lily for the first time this morning, when a young man jogged over to him—with basically the same expression Lily had when he'd first met her. He was no more than early twenties and tall and thin with a flop of brown hair under a brown cowboy hat.

"You gonna sell the Wild Canyon?" the guy asked, squinting at him in the bright morning sunshine. "Harlan always said if you wanted to know something to come out and ask like a man, so that's what I'm doing." His hands were on his hips. Bit of a tough-guy stance.

He'd heard "Harlan always said" a lot today. "I'll be honest with you—I don't know what I plan to do. Right now, I'm taking care of business and getting a feel for the ranch."

The guy glared at him. "If Harlan knew you were gonna sell his ranch, he'd rise from his grave and haunt you. No doubt."

Gavin raised an eyebrow. Just who was this kid? He was dressed for work as a cowboy and clearly had known Harlan, so he assumed he was a ranch hand.

"I actually believe in ghosts," Gavin said. "So I don't appreciate that. You work at the ranch?"

The guy slightly tilted his head as if he hadn't expected Gavin's response. "I'm Jonah Barnes. I'm a ranch hand and mostly herd cattle and ride fence. I'm gonna be working with Lily and a few others on running the animal sanctuary. We just got the two goats. Felix and Dodie. They're in their pen jumping on logs."

Ah. If Lily had chosen to work with him at her special sanctuary, she must like and trust the guy. Gavin would give him some more room here. But the kid was pushing it.

"Harlan was my mentor," Jonah continued. "He said he saw a lot of himself in me and was letting me shadow him the past few months so I could learn the business of ranching. He said a serious rancher should know all facets of the operation."

Gavin nodded. "I agree. And I'm very sorry for your loss."

The long arms crossed over the narrow chest. "Are you?"

"What's that supposed to mean?"

Jonah kicked at the dirt. "Nothing. But you did inherit the whole place now that he's gone."

He was worried about his job, maybe. Could watch the attitude around the new boss—just sayin'—but Gavin understood. Young guy with some bluster, had been close to Harlan, and here comes the long-lost son to swoop in and take everything. Jonah was clearly worried, like all the employees, that Gavin would sell it to someone who only cared about it from a making-money perspective. Several of the employees he'd spoken to today had told him they were sure he'd take good care of the ranch no matter what because he was Harlan's family and the ranch was his history and his future.

Gavin just nodded politely at those kinds of comments, the notion that he'd been "Harlan's family" eating away at his gut.

"I'd better get back to work before you fire me," Jonah said, tilting his head as if waiting to see how Gavin was going to respond to his attitude.

Good plan, he thought. "Stop by my office today. I'd like to hear more about the mentorship between you and Harlan. If you and Harlan spent a lot of time together the past few months, you might have some valuable information or insights about how the ranch was run, and it was obviously run well."

He wasn't sure why he was extending this olive branch to this kid. Maybe he saw something of himself in Jonah—ten years ago. Including the attitude. Gavin had been burning to prove himself to anyone. He didn't have his father's name to live up to; he'd had to build his own name and that had been fine with him.

Jonah stared at him—definitely not expecting this reaction. "We spent most of our time working on the details of the new animal sanctuary. Just a few days before he died, Harlan said he wanted to do the sanctuary because he was a throwaway just like the old animals that get kicked to the curb."

Gavin froze. "A throwaway?" he repeated. "What did he mean by that?"

Jonah gave something of a shrug. "At first I thought he meant by you. His own son not wanting anything to do with him. That was before I knew that was on Harlan, actually. I asked him what he meant by throwaway and he said he was abandoned on a doorstep with a note that said only one thing—his name."

What? "Whose doorstep?" Gavin asked. "As a newborn?"

Jonah shrugged. "He wouldn't say anything more about it. I tried to ask again the next day, but he looked upset so I shut up fast. A couple days later, he was gone." Jonah's face tightened and he looked down at the ground. "I should probably get back to the sanctuary. I'm in charge of getting the llamas' bedding ready for the day after tomorrow."

"Well, we'll talk again about continuing the mentoring, if you'd like."

Jonah eyed him. "Okay." And then he hurried away.

The conversation had left him unsettled, so when he saw Lily coming up the path in a peach pantsuit, floral scarf and a wide-brimmed straw hat, she was just what he needed. She stopped to talk to Jonah for a moment, then they both continued in their opposite directions.

"I hear the sanctuary goats arrived," Gavin said. "Felix and Dodie."

"Harlan named them when I first told him about them. Don't know where he plucked those names from, but they suit the old cuties. Did Jonah come to talk to you?"

"Talk at me, you mean? Yes. Since he's working with you on the sanctuary, I assume he generally presents himself better than he did with me?"

Lily gave a rueful smile. "He's always a bit grumpy, but he's been down since Harlan passed. He's a hard worker and really cares about animals."

"He mentioned that Harlan was mentoring him on ranch business. And that Harlan said he'd agreed to the sanctuary because he understood what it was like to be a throwaway—that he was abandoned on a doorstep."

Lily stared at him, confusion in her eyes. "What? Jonah never told me that."

"He said he tried to ask Harlan more about that but Harlan seemed upset so he let it go, and then Harlan died just a couple days later. Maybe Jonah figured he shouldn't be talking about it. I think he only told me because he blurted it out in anger. He's worried I'm going to sell the place. Said Harlan's ghost would haunt me if I did."

"Yup, that sounds like Jonah Barnes, all right," Lily said. "What'd you say to that?"

"That I believe in ghosts and didn't appreciate the remark. And that I'd like to talk more about the mentoring relationship."

Lily smiled—knowingly. "Yesterday I'd have been surprised that you didn't fire him on the spot. But now I know better. You place value in understanding people."

"He's just a kid."

"And you're just a nice guy, Gavin Dawson. Admit it."

He wouldn't describe himself as nice. Fair, sure. But a nice guy probably wouldn't sell the Wild Canyon out from all these people, particularly Lily and her family. Gavin could accept that he owned his late father's ranch, that he was carrying forth his legacy like it or not, and settle in on the gorgeous, thriving property and make it his own. He certainly knew how to do that. But it wasn't that simple.

All he had to do was think of the phone call his mother had made to Harlan. How nervous she must have been. The lie Harlan had told about a vasectomy. A click in her ear. All his burning questions and the terrible hot shame he'd felt when he had to face facts that his own father wanted nothing to do with him. Being a fatherless kid in a small town was the pits, and if Gavin ever had issues with other kids, that was the first place they went. *You don't have a father, loser.*

"Heard you met my mother and grandmother, by the way," she said. "They didn't bombard you with questions, did they?"

He smiled. "Nope. They did tell me to come early for lunch and they'd make me a special bowl of chili and give me still-warm corn bread. Think I'll do that. Join me? I have some questions—about the ranch and otherwise." He wanted to talk more about Harlan and the doorstep, though Lily hadn't even known about the doorstep. Had Harlan been adopted?

"Sure," she said, but he caught the hesitation.

Because of the kiss.

"Just taking my administrative assistant to lunch," he said. "On my first full day at work."

"Well, when you put it like that. Let me just lock up the office and note on the whiteboard I'll be at the caf."

He watched her slowly make her way up the steps. She stopped on the porch for a moment, gripping the railing, then locked the door and jotted the note on the board. When she turned back around, there was tension in her face.

"Lily? You okay?" he asked, hurrying over to her.

She grimaced and grabbed at her belly. "I had a strange pain—a sensation, really. Then another. Am I in labor? Was that a contraction? A false contraction? Just when I need to remember what I learned at Lamaze class, my mind is blank. Ow."

"Okay, I'm taking you to your doctor," he said, gently holding her arm and leading her down the steps and over to his truck.

She puffed out a few breaths and nodded. "Right on Main Street. Wait," she said, holding the door handle. "The tightening sensation seems to be gone. Oh wait, it's back. Ow," she added.

She wasn't kidding when she'd said she could go into labor any minute.

Maybe even in his truck.

After being squeezed in at her ob-gyn for an emergency appointment, Lily got the news that she was having common false contractions, Braxton-Hicks, and that she could rest assured she wasn't in early labor and the everything was okay. She was actually a little disappointed, since the possibility that she'd get to meet her baby almost two weeks early had gotten her excited. And scared.

Scared about being on her own, no partner. No father to care about Micah as much as she did. No emotional support from the other half of her family unit. The only other half of that family unit would be seven pounds, something ounces. Everything would be on her to ensure the well-being of this new life she was bringing into the world.

You have your mom and grandmother. They'll help you and you know that. You're gonna be fine, she reminded herself.

Now she and Gavin stood outside her doctor's office. She'd texted her mom that she'd gone into town with Gavin over some false contractions and that everything was A-OK and they'd have lunch here.

Her mother sent back two heart emoji and a winky face.

Okay, Mom. No matchmaking. First of all, Gavin Dawson wasn't romantically interested in a woman who really could give birth any second.

So then why had he kissed her last night? Technically, she'd leaned in first and he'd followed through. But really followed through. There was nothing chaste about that kiss. Nothing boss-admin. It was…hot.

Which all reminded her that she was standing outside her doctor's office with that new boss, who might be a great guy, but one she couldn't count on not to sell the ranch out from her under, taking all her security. Her home that she loved. The ranch that she loved. All the programs and initiatives, like the free equine-therapy course that little Acadia had joined. Her brand-new animal sanctuary, which was just getting going. Friends. Her family. Her mother and grandmother loved working in the cafeteria, their lives so much richer for it.

And it wasn't just the thought of losing the ranch that had her so out of sorts.

When they'd arrived at the doctor's office and Gavin had gone over to the reception desk to explain her situation, Lily had lowered herself onto a wide seat, her gaze going straight to the other women in the waiting room. To their left hands. And to the person sitting beside them. She'd tried to stop herself from doing this over the past months, but she couldn't seem to.

Lily was always the only one with her mom or her grandmother at her appointments. Everyone else was with a significant other, wedding rings gleaming. And there she'd been a bit earlier, worried about the strange tightening in her belly, and who was beside her? Not her husband. Not her baby's father. Not a great love.

Her scary new boss.

Scary yet kind and thoughtful and compassionate. After all, he'd brought her here without a second's hesitation or thought to his own schedule. He'd dropped everything.

She'd thanked him profusely on the way out of

the doctor's office, and he'd said, *Anything you need, Lily, anytime. You can count on that.*

That was all she really wanted in a life partner. A husband. A father for her child. Someone she could count on. For anything, anytime.

Which made her think of the kiss again. And what a good man he was. Good man and a good kisser.

She inwardly sighed. *You can't be attracted to him!* she yelled at herself. *You can't be.*

"So what are you craving for lunch?" he asked.

"I could really go for a greasy, gooey grilled cheese. Mmm, yes, now that I've said it, I must have it."

"Sounds good to me. Bear Ridge Diner?" he asked, pointing across the street where the favorite town eatery was at the end of the block.

She nodded. "Perfect. And maybe fries. In gravy."

"I could go for that too," he said. "Though I'm missing your mom and grandmother's chili and the still-warm corn bread."

"Oh, there's a lot more where all that came from," she assured him. "Not only did you come back to the ranch with me yesterday and sign a million things, but you dropped everything to take me here. Trust me, they'll whip you up specials all the time now."

They headed across the street to the diner. The place wasn't too crowded since the lunch crowd didn't get going until twelve thirty. Lily could forget about squeezing her belly into a booth, so they opted for a table in the back.

Danielle, the hostess, beat them there with a cushion for Lily's seat.

"You are the best," Lily said to her with a grin, getting herself onto the chair.

Which of course Gavin held steady for her. Once she was settled, he sat down.

Lily felt eyes on her and glanced around. A few people were staring their way and looking at Gavin.

"I hear that's Harlan Mandeville's son," she heard sixty-seven-year-old Edgar Willmers say at the counter to the waitress. Edgar was hard of hearing and tended to shout.

"I wouldn't know," Amanda, the waitress, responded, then fled to the end of the counter.

"Harlan had a son?" a woman two seats down from Edgar whispered. But Lily had heard her.

So had Gavin.

"Small town," he said. "I expect to be the hot gossip for a little while."

"You don't mind? I was the hot gossip when I first started showing. Everyone speculating who my baby's father was. I hated that. Do you believe that someone asked if Harlan was my 'baby daddy'? I almost slugged her!"

Gavin grimaced. "You should have."

"People should mind their own beeswax," she said.

He nodded. "That's hard for everyone. Take me, for example. I want to know Harlan's story. He was left on a doorstep?"

"Well, that's not gossip. That is your business. He's your father. And his family history is your family history."

"I still don't think of it that way. I grew up believing firmly that family and DNA weren't necessarily synonymous. Family is there. Family steps up. Family is about commitment and responsibility. What Harlan did was the opposite. He's not my family."

"I do understand," she said. "But you are interested in his family history. So forget about the stuff that bothers you and just focus on finding out what you want to know."

He smiled. "So ignore what I want and take what I want."

"Yes. Sometimes that's just the way it has to be."

The waitress came over and took their orders. Two gooey grilled cheeses, Lily's with apple slices, which she insisted was a family recipe and was an irresistible combination, and one big order of fries in gravy for them to share. Two iced teas.

"I'm trying to think of the best resource for finding out more about Harlan's family," he said. "Someone's gotta know something. A baby left on a doorstep seventy years ago."

The waitress brought their iced teas and Lily took a sip.

"I don't think he was born in Bear Ridge," she said. "Like you said, there are no Mandevilles in town."

"Or in the county," he said. "I did check."

"I remember you said that. Hmm. We could just try googling 'baby left on doorstep seventy years ago' and see what might pop up. That had to be a big news story."

He nodded and pulled out his phone and tapped away. "'Baby left on doorstep. Brewster County, Wyoming. Seventy years ago.'" He scrolled down the screen.

"Any hits?"

"No. Nothing. I'll type in his name and 'Wyoming' and see what comes up." He typed and then slid his finger up the small screen. "Just some news pieces about the ranch or something he said at a rancher-association meeting. Ah, here's something interesting. An interview in *Wyoming Rancher* magazine from fifteen years ago. Harlan was asked if ranching was in his blood. 'The wealthy rancher replied that some questions were better left as mysteries. So all we know is for twenty years, the Wild Canyon in Bear Ridge has been one of the most prosperous ranches in the county. No mystery there—Harlan Mandeville oversees all aspects of the business and personally hires all his staff.'"

The waitress brought over a tray with the grilled cheese and a big plate of gravy-covered fries. Yum. Lily grabbed a fry. Ahhh. Definitely hit that craving.

But suddenly her appetite waned. "Who would leave a baby on a doorstep?"

"His mother must not have been able to care for him. Maybe it was the doorstep of a wealthy family or a church."

She took a bite of her grilled cheese. "I wonder if he ever found his birth family. Given how closed off he was, how private, something tells me he didn't—didn't even pursue it. But that's just speculation. I really wouldn't know."

"I'll bet you're right, actually. He didn't want to know his own child, no curiosity, nothing. So I doubt he was interested in his birth family." He shook his head. "If I were him, I'd want to know. If I hadn't known my father's identity, I would have tried to track him down somehow, pestered my mother with questions until I got something to go on."

"Maybe Harlan found out something he didn't want to know. But again, speculation."

"I'm not entirely sure I want to know either," Gavin said, putting his sandwich down.

Edgar Willmers came over to the table, his young great-grandson beside him. "Are you really Harlan Mandeville's son?" he said to Gavin.

"I am," Gavin said.

"Well, I'll be. Harlan always said he wasn't going to continue the family name since it was made-up."

"Made-up?" Lily asked, eyes wide. "What do you mean?"

"I don't know," Edgar said. "That's just what Harlan told me one time. I once asked him what kind of name Mandeville was, that it sounded like royalty or something. And he snorted and said, 'Royalty, that's a laugh,' then said the name was made-up and walked away."

"Made-up," Gavin repeated. "He ever say anything else about it?"

Edgar shook his head. "Anytime I ran into him in town, which wasn't often, I'd ask him how he got his name, why it was made-up, what he meant by that, and he'd just wave his hand at me like he didn't want to talk about it and stalk off. I stopped asking years ago."

"Gramps, we have to get home by three," the teenaged boy beside him said.

"I'm coming, I'm coming," Edgar huffed.

Gavin watched the man leave. "A made-up name. So the people who took him in didn't adopt him, didn't give him their name? He was just randomly named Harlan Mandeville?"

"Sure sounds like it. Unless Edgar has it wrong. He's been very forgetful lately."

"Ah. Not sure how anyone would pull 'Harlan Mandeville' out of a hat. Not John Parker. Not Clint Jones. Not Pete McCann or something simple. Harlan Mandeville. That name must have meant something to whoever picked it. Might be our way to find out more."

She nodded. "Definitely. And I think it's good that you're interested, Gavin. It just might help put some things to rest."

"I don't know about that. Sometimes looking into the past leads to crud a person didn't need or want to know."

Lily gobbled up another fry drenched in craving-satisfying gravy. She was sure that finding out where he'd come from, through Harlan, would be good for him. Ninety-percent sure.

Chapter Five

"I think you should start your maternity leave when we get back to the Wild Canyon," Gavin said as he drove them to the ranch. No way should Lily, at nine months pregnant, be walking up and down the porch steps, getting up and down from her chair, even with her two cushions, and focusing on the running of the Wild Canyon and everyone else's needs but her own.

"Nah," she said, pushing her swirl of long blond hair, in its trademark low clip, behind her shoulders. "I've got two weeks to go. I'm not that uncomfortable. I'm fine to work another week. Help you get acquainted with the ranch."

He glanced at her. Not that uncomfortable? He'd think she'd want to start her time off. "If I need you, I'll text you, Lily. You live right on the property."

"No, really, that's all right," she said, a bit of edge in her voice. "Like I mentioned, my maternity pantsuits are very comfortable and giving," she said, patting her belly.

He could see her straining to smile and pulled over on the side of the road, putting the truck in Park.

"Why'd you stop?" she asked.

He shifted his body to face her. "Why do you want to keep wearing business suits so badly? Please be honest."

She sighed. "Fine. I want to be close by. Like right-outside-your-office close by. I need to know what's going on, Gavin."

He tilted his head. "I'm not following."

She stared out the window, then down at her belly and then finally at him. "The Wild Canyon is everything to me. My home. My way of earning a living. My family works there. I've got good friends who care about me, who I care about, all over the ranch. If you sell…" She turned away.

Ah. Now he understood. She was afraid he was going to upend her life.

He stared out at the Wyoming countryside on

both sides of this stretch of road, then turned to her. "What if I make you a deal, Lily Gold?"

Her blue eyes were still worried but curious. "What kind of deal?"

"What if I promise that I won't make any decisions about the ranch—what I plan to do—until the baby comes?"

"You'd make that promise?"

He nodded. "This is no time for you to be all stressed out, Lily. If my promising takes that worry off your shoulders, then done."

How had he come to care about this woman in such a short amount of time? Was it the pregnancy? That she was on her own and reliant on the ranch? That he could do for her what no one had done for his mother?

Or was it more than that? Like…what had led to that kiss in the nursery. Of all places.

She was quiet for a moment, then said, "So the day Micah is born you might sell?" The strain was back on her face. She shook her head. "You can't promise, Gavin. It's kind of you to wait until the big event, but the big event will be ongoing. I'll be out of commission for at least six weeks after the birth. So I do appreciate it, but—"

"Eight weeks total then," he said. "Cowboy's honor."

Her mouth dropped open. "Really? Why would you do that for me?"

"Because you've kept this place going behind the scenes since Harlan got too sick to make any decisions," he said. "I know that from going over the past few weeks of reports from the foreman and invoices. Harlan left you in charge of the office—the whole operation, really."

And because you've got some kind of hold on me.

"Well, I know it inside and out," she said. "Between me and the foreman, we got things done. Until we couldn't without your say-so."

"So let me do this for you," he said. "And I shouldn't sound like it's all about you. It'll force my hand to really get to know the ranch before I decide what I want to do with it. I'll have to live and breathe this place for eight weeks since the woman who knows it inside and out, as you said, will be otherwise engaged."

She laughed. "With motherhood and taking back my body."

"Exactly."

"And you'll have the time to find out about Harlan's past," she said. "Your past."

He put the truck in Drive and pulled back onto the road, slipping on his black sunglasses. "We'll see."

"I always think 'we'll see' is always a yes."

He smiled. "I wish I had half your optimism."

"I wasn't always the look-on-the-bright-side type. I do it for the baby. If I dwelled on what happened with his father or that there is no father, I'd be mopey. I don't want to be."

Interesting. Mood wasn't easy to fake. She must have really made the decision to look forward instead of back. That was admirable.

"If I could see the ranch as separate from Harlan, that would help," he said. "But I can't."

She nodded. "I do think of the baby as mine. The Ghoster isn't part of the equation anymore since he's long gone. I get how it's different for you." She glanced out the window, then back at him. "Did you ever think of having your own ranch?"

"Nope. I like traveling. I like turning ranches around, having a couple weeks' break and then moving on to another."

She seemed to be taking that in. Most people who asked him about his work didn't get how he lived on other people's ranches or hotels for months on end, no home base at all.

"Do you think it's about acceptance?" she asked. "As in, you're having a hard time accepting that Harlan left you his ranch when you don't feel any connection to him? I guess in my case,

I accept that I'm on my own with the baby. No husband, no partner, no one who'll love the baby as much as I do. No other half. At Lamaze class every week, at the doc's office, everywhere I go concerning the baby, I'm always with my mom. Not that I don't thank God for her. But today, when we were leaving the doc's office and I knew everything was okay, I walked out with someone who might be mistaken for the baby's father for the first time. And I liked it."

He'd once overheard his mother whispering to another waitress at her weekend job about being a single mother. He was supposed to be working on his math homework at the end of the counter, sipping on a milkshake and awaiting his burger. *Being a single mother in a really small town is hard enough. Having folks know I wasn't even married is harder. Either someone left me or I left someone for being no good. Either way people figure it, I'm stared at and judged, and it makes feel ashamed, when that's not fair...*

"I get it," he said. "You accept it, but it's hard."

"Yeah. And I get the baby. You get the ranch. Try to look at it like that. It's not about how you got here. Just that you're here. And the future."

Except the ranch was Harlan Mandeville. Everything about it.

"You always give me a lot to think about, Lily,"

he said. Not that he wanted to mull all that over. He'd tried looking at his situation a different way, but it always came back to Harlan being a bastard. The Wild Canyon being everything to the bastard. What the hell would Gavin want with it?

Except now it was also Lily's everything. Her exact words.

She squeezed his hand and then turned to look out the window, her hand back on her belly.

All he wanted in that moment was to pull the truck over again and hug her.

When they got back to the office, Buddy raced up to the car, his tail wagging happily. Lily noted how Gavin knelt down in front of the dog and gave him attention and hearty pats and scratches. That was very promising. Someone whose heart couldn't be reached or nabbed wouldn't be rubbing a stray border collie's belly while the pup stretched out on his back in the sun, and saying, "Who's a good boy?"

She was constantly noticing these little things—and the big ones, of course, like how he'd transported her to the doctor, how he was holding off on making any plans for the ranch until she was officially back from her leave. Eight weeks in total.

Plenty of time for Gavin Dawson to grow to love the ranch. To live and breathe it, as he'd said.

For it to get inside him. The land, the house, the employees—the Wild Canyon would become home in every way to him. The more he learned about Harlan's past, which sounded heart tugging, the more he'd let go of the bitterness he'd held inside him his entire life. Lily thought so, anyway. There was a lot to learn about his family history, and there was a good chance that the research would make him feel connected to Harlan and to the Wild Canyon.

That was Lily's big hope.

Unless Gavin was too detached or solitary or whatever the word was. A loner. A traveling executive cowboy who'd never wanted his own ranch. Or home. Or family. There was a good chance of that too.

So be careful, Lily. Your baby's father didn't tell you he had no plans to stick around after the weekend. Gavin Dawson is telling you to your face that he could not only leave but sell the ranch.

Don't forget that. Don't ever lose sight of it.

Do not fall in love with this man.

She bent over as much as she could to give Buddy a pat, then smiled at Gavin and headed for the steps to the office. She slowly made her way up. Not going up and down these stairs for a while would be just fine with her. That her apartment was one story was a huge plus. He hurried past her to open the door and hold it for her. She liked his chivalrous ways. A lot.

While Gavin went inside his office with a fresh mug of coffee that he'd insisted on making himself—Harlan Mandeville hadn't even known how to use the coffee maker—Lily got to work. On finding her replacement for her leave. Now that she knew she was safe, that the ranch was safe, for at least the next eight weeks, she could bring someone else in, train them this week on the basics. If Gavin needed her or anyone else did, she'd be right there, next door in her apartment. Another reason keeping her home was so important to her. One story, no running up and down stairs with a newborn in her arms, from the nursery to the kitchen. And when her leave was over, she'd be a few steps' commute away from the office.

She'd talk to Gavin about bringing Micah to work. She had a good feeling he'd be okay with that. Her mom and grandmother, excitedly counting down the days now, had said they'd watch their new baby relative during their off-hours. Maybe Gavin would even think about a ranch day care. Something she could propose. Quite a few of the employees had young children, and day care was expensive.

Just as she was about to craft an ad for the leave-replacement job or possibly call the employment agency in Brewster, the county seat and a bigger, more bustling town than sleepy Bear Ridge, Gavin came back out, coffee in hand.

He took a sip. "Hire an assistant for the assistant, if you'd like. You might be a whiz admin, even more so after ten years here, but a temporary maternity leave replacement won't be. Perhaps someone to do the grunt work for her or him a few days a week. Whatever you think."

"That's very thoughtful, Gavin," she said. Falling just a little bit in love with the man when she'd just told herself not to.

"Great coffee, by the way," he added, then headed back inside his office.

She shook her head in wonder. The parts of Harlan Mandeville that were wonderful and kind and generous—his son had definitely inherited those traits.

Lily spent the next fifteen minutes writing up the ad for the *Bear Ridge Gazette* and the employment agency, then typed out a job posting for the assistant to the assistant and tacked it beside the whiteboard on the office door.

A rap on the door had her turning to find Jonah there.

"Hi, Jonah. How are Felix and Dodie settling in?" she asked.

Jonah smiled, a rare sight these days. "Felix

loves the log in his pen. Dodie likes to just stare at him on it. They've eaten, and I gave them both a slice of apple, so now I'm their favorite. Sorry."

Lily laughed. "I'll be the llamas' favorite. I can't wait to meet them."

"Me too." He glanced toward Gavin's closed office door. "So I was wondering if Gavin might have time to talk to me—about the mentoring."

"Let me buzz him." She pressed the intercom on the landline. Gavin answered, his voice sounding so sexy. "Jonah Barnes is here if you have some time to talk about continuing the mentorship program."

"Sure, send him in," Gavin said.

She was about to tell Jonah to go right in when Aria Gallo, one of their cowgirls and a great all-around ranch hand, came in. Her eyes went straight to Jonah, who turned a bit red and stared down at his feet. Hmm, something between them?

"Lily, do you have a moment?" Aria asked. She was nineteen and so mature for her age. When Aria had interviewed for the full-time cowgirl position, she'd been so impressed by the young woman's poise. Aria was tall and slender like Jonah, with long dark hair she wore in a trade-mark braid and dark sparkling eyes.

"Sure," she said, then looked at Jonah. "Go right in, Jonah."

He dashed to the door like he couldn't get away from Aria fast enough.

Interesting.

He disappeared inside the office and shut the door.

"What can I do for you, Aria?" Lily asked, gesturing at her guest chair.

Aria sat. "The reason I came is to ask if I can shift my station to the animal sanctuary full-time since I'm so excited about it. But I also just saw the job posting on the whiteboard for the temporary assistant to your maternity leave assistant, and I could really use some extra hours. Can I apply?"

Lily's eyes widened. Aria had worked every summer as an office girl for her dad's accounting practice all through high school. She'd be perfect for the assistant job.

"I put that posting up not fifteen minutes ago," she said with a grin. "I'll go take it down. Assistant to the assistant—check. Thanks for taking one thing off my keep-track-of list."

Aria beamed. "Great! Thank you so much!"

"And yes, you can switch your station to the animal sanctuary. I like the idea of having dedicated staff there. You, Jonah and two other hands have expressed interest."

"It's my lucky day, for sure," Aria said. "I can't wait to meet the llamas the day after tomorrow!"

Lily smiled. "Jonah just said almost that exact thing."

Aria's eyes turned a bit dreamy for a moment. Someone definitely had a crush.

"You can start tomorrow in the office," Lily said. "Come over at eleven. That'll give you time at the sanctuary and a break. I'll show you what's what, and then when the new admin eventually arrives, you can jump right in."

"Perfect." Aria stood and glanced at Gavin's closed door. "Jonah's not quitting, is he?"

Lily shook her head. "They're talking about continuing the mentorship program that Harlan started."

"Really? Jonah seemed really grumbly about the new owner. Is he nice?"

"Super nice," Lily said.

Aria glanced at the door. "Maybe Jonah will come out any second and we can walk back to the sanctuary together. I signed up to work there this afternoon. The goats are so cute."

"They really are." She glanced at Aria, who kept looking at the door, very clearly willing it to open and for Jonah to come out. "Are you and Jonah dating?" she whispered.

"I wish," she whispered back. "But I don't think he likes me that way. We talk for like two seconds and he finds some excuse to leave."

"He's on the shy side," Lily said.

"I'd ask him out but I'd be mortified if he turned me down. That would be so awkward since we're both gonna be working at the sanctuary."

"I get it. But maybe the reason he makes himself scarce around you is because he does like you that way. If he was neutral, there'd be no issue, you know?"

Aria brightened. "I didn't think of that. Hmm. Maybe I will ask him out."

"You do that," Lily said.

Aria left with a big grin. *Look at you, matchmaking*, she told herself. Jonah could use a girlfriend, that was for sure. And Aria was a lovely person. Lily could absolutely see them together.

When Aria left, Lily looked at her to-do list for the afternoon and realized how right Gavin was about her starting her leave pretty much now. She barely had the energy to even look at the list. It was filled with some standard but tedious HR-related tasks, like going through all the emails and separating the invoices from the cattle auctions and rancher-association meetings.

She was pretty sure Harlan would have told her to start her leave and hire herself a replacement and an assistant, likely encouraged by hints from her mother and grandmother while he was in the caf for the daily lunch special. Harlan never missed a day, unless he had to be out of town. But her gaze kept going to Gavin Dawson's closed office door, wanting to see his handsome face and his long, lean, muscular body in his dark jeans and dress shirt and boots.

What was making her stomach all fluttery, aside from the obvious, was that she could see them together. A fantasy that would never become reality.

Chapter Six

Jonah was a fidgeter, a foot tapper, a leg-cross switcher, and it was driving Gavin slowly insane. He was also difficult to talk to. Gavin always remembered what one of his elementary teachers wrote on his report card. Getting Gavin to respond to questions during class discussions is like pulling teeth. Same could be said right now for Jonah.

"So what area of ranch operations were you and Harlan working on last?" he asked.

Jonah crossed his left foot over his right knee. Then switched again. "We were mostly talking about the sanctuary because he knew I was interested in that." He wasn't even trying for the usual pleasant-neutral expression.

Something was clearly bothering him.

"You and Harlan were close?" Gavin asked. As the kid had said, if you want to know something, just come out and ask like a man.

"As close as anyone can get to Harlan. You know how he is." He caught himself and shifted in his seat. "I guess you don't."

"It seems to bother you that I inherited the Wild Canyon when I wasn't at all a part of Harlan's life."

Jonah glanced at him then, clearly surprised Gavin had been so direct. "It does."

"Why? I mean, I can figure out the gist—that it seems unfair—but I sense there's more to it for you."

Jonah fidgeted some more and settled back in the chair, crossing his arms over his chest. "I thought Harlan would leave me something. I don't know what—his favorite Stetson, a brown one. His belt buckle that he wore to rancher-association meetings. A horse. Whatever. You know what he left me? Nothing."

Gavin studied him, seeing pain in the guy's eyes, not anger. "You feel overlooked by him? That it meant you weren't special to him?"

Jonah bolted up and swiped at his eyes; Gavin could see tears glistened, and this time there was anger. "I know Harlan liked me. He once said if he were a different kind of person, I'd be like a grandson to him. A grandson. And then he left me nothing, like I didn't matter to him at all."

"He didn't leave his administrative assistant of ten years anything either," Gavin pointed out. "And it's clear how he felt about Lily. So I don't think you should read anything personal into that."

"Well, how should I read it, then?" he asked with a glare, sinking back down in his chair. "It made me really mad at him. And that was tearing me up inside because I really cared about Harlan. I never had someone in my life like him. No one thought I'd amount to anything or cared if I did. My father's an alcoholic who's been in and out of jail for years, and my grandfather was the same till he died. I'm not gonna continue the family tradition."

His home life had to have been rough. "I have no doubt of that," Gavin said. "You have goals and drive and ambition or you wouldn't have been Harlan's mentee. You wouldn't have come talk to me."

Jonah seemed to calm down some.

"As far as Harlan's will," Gavin continued, "I think he left everything to me because he felt he had to make amends somehow, and that taking one thing away, the smallest thing like his favorite Stetson or a cabin or his belt buckle, would take something away from me. And maybe he figured he'd done enough of that his whole life."

Jonah tilted his head and Gavin could see he was thinking that over. "I heard he never even paid child support. Just acted like he didn't have a kid out there. Is that true?"

"Yup. You know that because he said so or you heard it around?"

"Heard it around. Once word got out that he had a son who inherited the ranch, everyone was talking. I guess a couple people knew your mom from way back, but they said they just thought it was a rumor that Harlan was the dad, like maybe she wanted to pin it on someone rich."

Gavin bristled at the mention of his mother. She didn't pin her pregnancy on anyone.

"Harlan would only tell me that he'd made mistakes he wouldn't have undone but still felt crappy about," Jonah said. "I don't really get that."

Gavin did. Harlan Mandeville was a crappy person. Period. All the free programs at the ranch for kids and senior-animal sanctuaries wouldn't change that.

He leaned back in his chair. He could say that all he wanted. But it did change things. Everything he'd been learning about Mandeville added up to someone who did care about people and animals.

"I guess it means he knew himself," Gavin said.

"He'd make his mistakes all over again because that's who he was—limited in whatever area the fatherly gene comes from—but he understood it was wrong and it did haunt him, I guess. To use your word."

Yeah. Gavin was pretty sure he had that right. Harlan had been haunted by what he'd done. So he'd left his ignored long-lost son everything he had. The Wild Canyon.

Jonah glanced up at him then. "You hate him?"

"Sometimes. Over the years, I'd go from hating him or thinking he just must have been limited so I couldn't blame him, and that would help me feel better about it, that it wasn't his fault because he wasn't capable of more. But then I'd go back to hating him. Step up, man. Try. Find it in yourself." He shook his head.

"I end up feeling bad when I hate my dad," Jonah said. "I always think—he could stop drinking if he really gave two figs about me. But then I think, no he can't. That's why he's an alcoholic. He tried rehab a few times but it never stuck." He looked out the window, such strain in his young face.

"My cousins—they own the Dawson Family Guest Ranch in town. Their father was a raging alcoholic. It took them a long time to come to terms with how it affected them. If you ever want to talk to any of them, I could set that up. Ford and Rex are both cops at the BRPD. You've probably seen them around town."

"Yeah, I know who they are. Ford Dawson arrested my dad the last time he went to jail. I'm listed as next of kin since my mom's remarried, so he actually came to talk to me. He seemed all right."

"He is. He's a good resource for you, Jonah. Know you can talk to him anytime."

Jonah nodded and looked away again, then down at his lap. "You know what I don't get about Harlan? I can't imagine having a kid and never seeing him or caring about what happens to him. My dad? Yeah, I get it. But yours was the richest guy in town, and your mom had to work two jobs, I heard."

Gavin nodded. "So now you get the full picture why I'm ambivalent about the place. There's a lot behind the inheritance and absolutely nothing."

Jonah stared at him, taking that in. Gavin knew the kid had walked into the office angry and would be leaving with more to think about than he'd counted on.

"I'd like to continue the mentorship program with you if you're interested," Gavin said. "From the reading I've done, most internships like this lead to an assistant foreman job. Are you interested in that path?"

"Actually I'm not sure. The foreman job is mostly managing stuff. I want to do work with the animals, you know?"

"You could specialize in an area—cattle, horses. And work up to running that operation. You can still be out there, just in charge."

Jonah beamed. "That's more my speed. I could run the cattle operation someday?"

"Well, that's managing too. But you might find you like that. It's just figuring out the right and best way to get things done for the herd. It's not boring number crunching."

Jonah perked up. "Oh. Well, in that case, sign me up."

Gavin smiled and extended his hand. "We'll focus on the cattle, then, but include all areas of ranch operation when we meet."

Jonah stood up. "This went better than I thought. I was pretty sure you were gonna throw me out on my butt." He glanced toward the door. "Could you do me a favor? Not a big-favor favor, just a lookout thing."

Gavin tilted his head. "What do you mean?"

"Could you poke your head out and see if Aria is still with Lily? I'm sort of trying to not run into her."

The young woman who'd been with Lily when Gavin had entered his office? "Aren't you two working together at the sanctuary?"

"Yeah, but there I know how to talk to her. I just talk about the animals and what snacks goats like and how many stomachs llamas have. But when I see her around the ranch, nothing comes out of my mouth and I seem like a total freak."

Gavin smiled. "Yeah, I've been there. You know you could talk to her about the sanctuary if you see her around the ranch. Just as a starting point. Something funny a goat did. That sort of thing."

"I try but the words get stuck in my throat. She's just too pretty. And smart. And interesting. And what's the point, anyway? Nothing lasts. Nothing."

Gavin knew that as a fact, but coming out of a twenty-year-old's mouth, a guy with his entire life ahead of him? Wrong. "Yeah, been there too. I get it. But you know that saying about it being better to have loved and lost than never to have loved at all?"

"Um, big disagree on that one," Jonah said. "It's better to not bother because there's no point. Harlan always said being practical would take me places."

Yeah, a straight road to loneliness. To nothing. To no one.

Like Harlan.

Like Gavin.

But maybe this all was a talk for another time.

"So will you see if she's gone?" Jonah asked.

Gavin went to the door and poked his head out, Lily turning his way.

Talk about too pretty. Those blue eyes and the one dimple in her right cheek. The glowing face.

The guest chairs were empty. He sat back down at his desk.

"Don't see her."

"Phew," Jonah said. "Well, thanks for everything today, Gavin. You're not so bad, after all."

Gavin laughed. "Always appreciate hearing that."

They shook hands and he walked Jonah to the door and opened it for him.

"See ya soon, Lily," Jonah said with a nod at her and headed out.

Lily smiled at him, then turned to Gavin. "He looked a lot happier than when he went in."

"Well, that's my job. My former job, I guess. Turning things around."

"I hope you turn yourself around, Gavin," she said, then clamped a hand over her mouth. "Did I say that aloud?" Her cheeks reddened. "I mean about the ranch. Making your peace."

He just looked at her for a moment and gave something of a nod, just an acknowledgment that she'd said something, and went back inside his office.

Now here he was, pulling a Jonah, unable to talk.

He wasn't so sure he had to turn himself around at all. His feelings were justified. Which reminded him of his mother, who used to love watching Dr. Phil on TV. She'd always say to people who felt they too were justified in this or that, *Yeah, you know you're right. But do you want to be right or do you want to be happy?*

Gavin didn't see much room for happiness where owning the Wild Canyon was concerned. Just a bunch of bitter-tinged memories.

As Lily got ready to leave for the day, she wondered if she should stop being so pushy. Sometimes she had to be; the job often demanded it. But in this case, with Gavin, she was talking about his personal life as much as his ownership of the Wild Canyon, and when it came to that blurred line, she should probably keep her lips zipped. Unless he asked, of course.

But then again, this involved her life too.

Thank heavens her friend Brianna was coming over tonight. They'd been close since junior high school, and Lily could confide in Bri. Her friend was due over at six with a large pizza, half spinach, half mushroom, and Lily couldn't wait to flop on the sofa, as much as she could flop, and have girl talk, pizza and her promised pedicure. Lily's days of polishing her own toenails had been over for months now.

She knocked on Gavin's door to let him know she was leaving for the day and see if there was anything else he needed. He said he was heading to the cafeteria for dinner to have that chili and corn bread and asked her to please stop working for the day.

Lily smiled and that was that, the office was closed. Except she wanted to linger, to ask him how it had gone with Jonah, to just be near him, to talk to him, to have his gorgeous green eyes looking at her. Sometimes he looked so confident, like the executive cowboy he was, the owner of this place, and sometimes, like now, he looked like he was a million miles away, thinking hard about something that was weighing on his mind.

But they both had to go. She hoped her mom and gram wouldn't bombard him with questions, particularly since he'd been her superhero today by whisking her off to the doctor. But she was sure they would. Tamara and Betsy had a way of putting people with scowls into good moods, so they'd likely work their warm, friendly, ask-personal-questions-in-the-right-way magic on him.

Once inside her apartment, she got out of her cowboy boots and headed into her bedroom to change into her comfiest lounge clothes. Ahhh. Tomorrow she'd definitely wear her stretchy dress to the office. The pantsuits, which always made her feel professional and a little taller, especially around troublesome types, had outlived their welcome now that she had her solid eight weeks to work her own brand of magic on Gavin Dawson. If she could.

The doorbell rang and Lily called out a "come in" so she wouldn't have to pull herself up from the sofa.

Bri came in with a huge pizza box. Lily could smell the delicious contents from her spot and her mouth watered. They spread out on the sofa, the pizza, plates and drinks on the coffee table in front of them. "So everything's really okay?" Bri asked, pulling her long red hair into a low ponytail. "I was so nervous when I got your text after you left your doctor's office this afternoon."

"Everything's fine. Baby Micah isn't coming early as far as my OB could tell. But she did say I should have my hospital bag packed and ready."

"Got everything in it you need? I could ask my sister back for what she's not using." Bri had two kids of her own, three and almost five, and her sister'd had a baby right before Lily found out she was pregnant, so she'd given all her expecting and newborn stuff to her sister.

"My mom and grandmother are very organized," she said with a grin. "They actually packed my hospital bag for me, then took out everything one by one for my approval. I have a big fluffy robe with pockets, big fluffy slippers, two kinds of lotion and ointments, and a sitz bath, not that I've read up too much on that. Two bags of my favorite sucking candy, three magazines, a stack of burp clothes and newborn diapers, a soft baby blanket embroidered with Micah's name, and a going-home outfit for both of us. There's much more, but I can't hold all that in my head."

Bri laughed. "Your mom and gram are the best."

"They really are. Except for right about now. I think they're interrogating Gavin Dawson in the caf over their chili and corn bread. Buttering him up to get him to talk."

"About…" she prompted, opening the pizza box and taking out a slice of mushroom.

Lily decided to start with spinach. She took a bite, the gooey cheese stretching from the slice. "Mmm. So good." She took another bite. "They want him to feel like the Wild Canyon is home, not a reminder of the father who didn't acknowledge him since he was born. Yeesh, when I say it that way…"

Brianna sipped her soda. "Do you think he could think of the ranch as home?"

"I honestly don't know. He's a ranching man and the place is beautiful, so it's possible. And it's my evil plan—to help him love the Wild Canyon so that selling is off the table."

"Well, the fact that he's at the caf right now is a good sign. If he wasn't interested in the ranch, he wouldn't be eating in the caf. He'd be at the Italian restaurant in town, having thirty-dollar pasta in truffle sauce."

"I wish he were that easy to box, but he's complicated. Huge heart on one hand. Stone wall on the other."

"You'll break through—you're Lily Gold," Bri said.

Lily grinned. "The nine months pregnant Lily Gold is exhausted, though. I feel like I gave everything I had to convincing Gavin to come out to the ranch. I might not have an ounce of energy left."

Bri's brown eyes twinkled. "Oh, I don't think that'll be a problem. 'Cause if I'm not reading you wrong, it's personal too. And I don't mean the ranch because it's home and your job and your whole life here. You like him. Like him, like him."

Lily couldn't help her smile and felt her head go slightly empty. There were times she thought about Gavin Dawson and got all dreamy the way she had in high school when she had crushes. The way she had when she'd met her child's father.

Which sobered her up some. She had to be careful with Gavin, careful with her hormonal feelings, careful with her heart, careful with a whole mess of important stuff she couldn't control.

"I do. I really like him. Just when I needed someone to lift me up, cut me a break, make me feel like everything is going to be okay because of this sudden interloper, he's the one doing all that good stuff." She thought of the body pillow he'd bought her. The sweet book with quotes and reflections on motherhood.

Brianna laughed. "I saw his photo on his website. He's also hot."

"Yup, that too. And a really great kisser."

Brianna's eyes widened. "You kissed? Tell me everything."

"Totally out of the blue. Apparently we were having a moment and both went with it—I leaned in first. And then it was over in five seconds and we both agreed it didn't happen. Couldn't happen again."

Brianna got that devilish twinkle in her eyes again. "As if anyone can pretend a kiss didn't happen."

"I learned that fast," Lily said, taking another bite of her delicious pizza.

"On a scale of one to ten, what's the possibility of you two getting together?"

"Either a one or a ten. That's how much I don't know." That kiss was going to happen again. Not much else could for a long time, though. At least during the weeks he was sticking around. Maybe that was a good thing. They would truly get to know each other during that time. Maybe he'd reveal himself to be the rotten egg she'd thought he was back when he was ignoring her texts and calls.

Yeah, right. The man was definitely a good egg. The best egg.

Brianna laughed. "Then the answer is ten, honey."

What was also diametrically opposed was how she wanted and didn't want that to be true at the same time. She was about to have a baby. Who starts a romance at nine months pregnant?

With a man who may or may not be sticking around.

Not a smart woman, that was for sure.

Chapter Seven

The moment Gavin walked into the cafeteria, all eyes swung his way and a hush came over the dinner crowd. He got it. He was the new owner and a big topic of conversation. Everyone was wondering the same thing—what he'd do with the ranch, if they could count on their jobs. When he went up to the line and waited like everyone else, grabbing a tray and glancing up at the chili special, which he was definitely getting, the caf went back to somewhat normal, people talking and eating. And likely he was the hot topic of their conversation.

"You're the new owner, right?" the middle-aged

cowboy in front of him said as he turned around. Two other cowboys with him turned too.

He nodded and extended his hand to the three men. "Gavin Dawson."

"Good to meet you. I'll tell ya, Harlan would never have waited in line for grub. He always went right up to the front. But he was a good man. I told Lily that my son needed braces and asked about overtime for the next two years, and do you want to know what Harlan did? He gave me a raise instead." There were murmurs from the two other guys and the people around them of what a decent man Harlan was.

Gavin's least favorite topic of conversation. What a great guy Harlan Mandeville was. "Sounds like he really cared about his employees." He made himself say the words. Though it did seem to be true. That also rankled.

He avoided the thought that popped in his head: not that he cared about his own flesh and blood. He was getting tired of that himself. Maybe that was a step in the right direction. Letting go of the bitterness, if that's what he was doing. Maybe the truth of his and Harlan's connection had just settled into him and he only had to work on accepting that the place was his now, home.

One of the other cowboys nodded. "I needed a divorce lawyer and couldn't pay for it and Harlan sent me to someone he knew. Turns out he took care of the entire cost. I asked him why and he said I did good work and marriage could ruin a man."

Marriage could ruin a man. Interesting. That motto hadn't come from Harlan's personal experience, because as far as Gavin knew, his father had never married. But he'd have to dig deeper than he had.

And there it was again. Harlan Mandeville being a saint to everyone except his own flesh and blood. So much for letting the truth of family history settle in. Mandeville helped everyone but the woman who was pregnant with his baby. And the son who grew up without a father.

He thought about what both Lily and Jonah had told him—that Harlan hadn't left them a thing in his will. Not a cent, not a Stetson, nothing. Two employees he seemed to especially care about. His theory on that, that Harlan probably felt that the son he'd turned his back on deserved the whole kit and caboodle, down to the last saddle, struck him as the right one.

But still, it was strange. How could he not leave the people closest to him, whom he cared for so deeply, anything? The man had been complicated, yes, but maybe even more complicated than Gavin had figured. He'd always thought it was a cut-

and-dried case of a cruddy person. But there was clearly more to it.

The why of the cruddy.

The questions would keep poking at him so he'd have to do his digging into Harlan whether he wanted to or not. His father was proving impossible to peg and pigeonhole, and Gavin did want to know what had made the self-made man tick.

Once he got up to the front of the line, Lily's mother, Tamara Gold, beamed at him and asked if he still wanted to try their award-winning chili that had gotten them first place at the county fair last summer. It was today's special, just $2.99 a bowl, including corn bread. Yes, he did.

The corn bread was still warm as promised earlier. He took his tray to a table in the back so that he'd have a good view of the entire room. The caf was inviting, and most people seemed to be having a good time. Very few people sat alone.

The chili was everything Lily's mother and grandmother had said it was. Hit the spot. He'd just about finished the bowl and the corn bread when the two petite blondes, who looked so much like each other and Lily, came over to his table in their Wild Canyon Ranch Caf aprons. Lily's mom carried a complimentary serving of chocolate coconut pie, which he'd always loved, and the women sat down to chat. At first they'd talked about the cafeteria, how it was run and that the employees loved the food, which he could understand. Then the conversation had turned to Lily and how thankful they were that he'd been right at her side when she'd started having those pains and rushed her to her doctor.

"Usually, the husband, the baby's father, would be the one to do that, so thank you," Betsy Parker, Lily's grandmother, said. "My dear daughter, Tamara, here, and I were so grateful that you whisked her right off."

"Of course," Gavin said. "I'm just relieved everything is okay."

"You swooped in like a knight in shining armor," Betsy said, touching a hand reverently to her chest. "Which is just what our Lily needs. Yes, she's perfectly capable on her own and feisty and her own woman. But someone to share the burdens and the joy? That's what she needs. Lily doesn't like being single," she added on a whisper, looking directly at him. "But we're working on that."

"Mom," Tamara warned. "I'm sure Lily doesn't want us sharing her personal life with her new boss."

"What is more personal than sitting with Lily in the waiting room of her ob-gyn?" Betsy asked and nodded pointedly. She turned to Gavin. "Lily is the best person on earth. She deserves to have a great love in her life, a partner to share in parent-hood with her. That's all I'm saying."

Gavin slipped a finger into the collar of his shirt and tugged at it. Was it hot in here? He didn't want to contemplate Lily's love life. The thought of her with a man beside her poked at his gut, but he wasn't sure why. He was protective of her, sure. But of course he wanted her to have all the good things in life.

He did recognize the pokes as a bit of jealousy, if he had to be honest. He and Lily had kissed, after all. So there was clearly something between them on that level, even if they'd both shelved it as in-appropriate given their work relationship. But not liking the idea of her falling for someone, when he definitely wanted her to be happy—that was off.

"I'm making up a dating profile for Lily for Wy-oming Love Match, the online service," Betsy said. "I can get away going behind her back in ways her mother can't. Helps to be the dear old granny."

"Mom! Stop telling the man every detail! And how is Lily supposed to date when she has a new-born? She'll literally have her hands full. And she won't be physically up to it."

"Her suitors will call on her in the living room," Betsy countered. "She'll sit on the sofa across from the gentlemen and they'll chat and she'll assess them as fathers and husbands."

"You do know what year it is, right, Mom?" Tamara asked, pressing the back of her hand to her mother's forehead.

Betsy grinned. "That gal is the sweetest and so beautiful and she's gonna be all alone with that baby. Yeah, she's got us. But she needs love and partnership and a father for her child. I know what I know."

"Maybe so," Tamara said. "But Lily's not going to be interested in a dating service."

Gavin took a bite of his pie, at first glad the conversation was going on around him and not with him. But he latched on to the last bit. "Lily isn't interested in finding this great love?" He found himself asking the question without exactly meaning to.

He was curious.

"Lily's a practical sort, but when it comes to love, she wants it to happen naturally," Tamara said.

"Phoo on that!" the grandmother bit out. "That's how she got in trouble with the guy who took off on her. She gave her heart to a schmuck. This way, we make sure the men she meets tick the boxes."

"Let's get through the birth and newborn stage before we worry too much about her love life, Mom."

Betsy shrugged and looked at Gavin long and hard. "Gosh, you two would make a lovely couple."

"I'm her boss," Gavin reminded her. "That puts me out of the running." But apparently not for thinking about her all the time. Wondering how she was feeling, if she needed anything.

"Hogwash," Gram said, those intelligent blue eyes of hers working away.

Luckily the two women were called up by one of the kitchen staff.

Lily with a suitor. A caller. A boyfriend. A husband. A man at her side to be her baby's father.

He felt his stomach churn at the thought.

You just want the best for her, he told himself, finishing up his pie.

Either that or he just plain wanted her.

As if having the big question of who the hell his father was—as a person—constantly weighing on his mind wasn't enough, now he had the thought of Lily's family working behind the scenes to find a husband for her and father for her baby. Each shoulder now had its own thousand-pound press.

On the way back from the cafeteria, he met more employees, shook more hands, tried to assure them that if he did sell the Wild Canyon, he'd be thoughtful about it, but that didn't exactly appease anyone, and he understood. He didn't know what he was going to do with the place. Still, the good people who worked for the ranch were living, breathing humans with needs and stories, and when he thought about just walking away, signing away the place, lately he was thinking of them.

And Lily.

But he was always thinking about Lily.

To get her off his mind, he decided to focus on Harlan Mandeville and finding some answers about his past.

Another thing he was doing lately: thinking about how Harlan's past was Gavin's past. Because no matter how much Gavin wanted to deny that they were connected in any way except for DNA, they were connected. DNA did mean something or Gavin wouldn't be so damned tied in knots over his paternity.

His father, who for years was one of the wealthiest ranchers in town and the county, had been left on a doorstep as a baby.

A doorstep.

By whom? And whose doorstep?

And why were there no Mandevilles in a hundred-mile radius of Bear Ridge? Something had drawn Harlan to the town. Bear Ridge was sleepy with its share of charm, but it was a small town in a rural area. Most people who lived here were from here. So had Harlan been left on a Bear

Ridge doorstep? Or had he closed his eyes and pointed at a map of Wyoming and where his finger landed, he'd start his ranch?

Gavin's entire life—his job as a ranching consultant, executive cowboy—was about finding answers. And he'd get them about his father. For once, the answers he sought were very personal.

He started in Harlan's office, where he'd already spent a lot of time since he'd arrived. But he'd been so busy studying the financials and the day-to-day operations and meeting with the foreman, who seemed like a great, trustworthy guy, that he hadn't gone looking through the files for anything marked Personal.

As he'd done since he'd made his way to the office five minutes ago from the main house, he kept peering out the door to see if Lily was around. She wasn't.

Not now either.

Or now.

If she wasn't nine months pregnant, if he hadn't had to tell her to start her leave right away, he'd make some work-related excuse to see her. But of course he couldn't do that.

You could simply inquire how she's doing, he reminded himself.

And he did want to know.

He looked out toward her desk again. No Lily.

Shaking his head at himself, he went to the door and closed it. He suddenly needed blinders when it came to a woman?

Sitting down at the big desk, he opened the bottom drawer with its neat letter-size hanging files. All to do with the ranch. Nothing personal in the credenza or the closet. He lifted all the paintings and framed illustrations to look for a hidden safe, but all he found was wall. No trapdoor under the area rug.

He left the office, all too aware he was hoping Lily would be out there, maybe getting herself some decaf even though she had a coffee maker in her apartment. She wasn't there.

He went out the main door and around to the front of the house, where Buddy was snoozing on the porch on the new memory foam dog bed Gavin had picked up yesterday. He stopped to pet him. Still no word from the shelter, veterinarian or lost-dog sites about anyone calling to claim him.

Which meant in a few days, Buddy would be his dog.

But I can't have a dog because I don't have a home.

He recalled Lily laughing the first time he'd said that. *You have a mansion*, she'd reminded him.

But maybe not for long. And then what? He'd sell the Wild Canyon and go back to his life on the road, taking Buddy with him? It was possible. But a lot for a dog to get used to a new place over and over. He'd have to think about this.

Gavin walked in the front door of the log mansion as he thought of it, and as usual stopped dead in his tracks to take in how gorgeous and grand the place was. The craftsmanship, the details, the furnishings. Luxe yet somehow rustic in a very polished way. He had to admit he loved the house, from the huge stone fireplace to the dark wood beams on the ceilings. The kitchen was state-of-the-art. Turned out a housekeeper came in twice a week to clean and to stock the freezer with meals, and when she'd asked if Gavin wanted to continue that arrangement, he'd opted for the cleaning but he actually liked to cook. He also liked the idea of eating in the cafeteria, which was a good way to observe the employees and get the hum of the ranch.

In the master bedroom, huge, masculine, with its king-size bed and dark brown leather headboard, the great view of the stables, he did a search for wall and floor safes. Nothing.

His personal papers had to be somewhere. A safe-deposit box, maybe. But the lawyer hadn't mentioned anything like that, and he would have. Gavin would call the guy in the morning and ask if Harlan had kept any personal documents with him.

If I find out who you were, it's not going to tell me who I am. I know who I am. My mother's son. A consulting rancher. A traveler.

And now the owner of the Wild Canyon. Harlan Mandeville's son. He couldn't ignore that anymore, separate those two details from himself. He didn't know if Lily was right, though. If digging into the past would help or settle anything. Harlan had turned his back on him, and anything he learned wouldn't make that right. How could it?

He dropped down on the bed and looked out the window. He hated when he couldn't make sense of his own thoughts, his own problems. He just kept going in circles when it came to his father.

He thought about what Jonah had said earlier. *Harlan would only tell me that he'd made mistakes he wouldn't have undone but still felt crappy about. I don't really get that.*

Gavin did get it. Which was interesting. Did he really want to understand Harlan Mandeville? He could think of a few relationships he'd had with women where he'd ended up breaking a lovely heart and he'd felt terrible about it, but he wouldn't have handled the romance or the break-up any differently.

Dammit.

He headed back downstairs and outside, Buddy following as he went around the side of the house to the office entrance on the off chance Lily was there, though he was the one who'd told her to not be there.

He was losing it.

A piece of white paper was taped to the whiteboard.

LOST DOG. Arlo. Black-and-white border collie mix. Someone said they mighta seen him around the house.
Bill in the old cabin.

Gavin reread the sign, which was scrawled in black pen, then looked down at Buddy.

"Arlo?" he said to the dog, who immediately wagged his tail and looked at him with bright, alert eyes as if finally someone was calling him by the right name. "Arlo, huh?" He knelt down and scratched the dog under the chin. The tail wagged away. Gavin was 99 percent sure the pooch was smiling.

Arlo. Not Buddy.

What was this pang in his chest? He should be glad that Buddy—Arlo—had a home, that someone was looking for him. Someone named Bill in the old cabin, whatever and wherever that was.

The perfect excuse to go see Lily.

Chapter Eight

Lily stood in front of the crib in the nursery, her heart almost bursting at the sweet pale yellow bedding with its faint white stars. Her mother and grandmother had furnished the nursery as a surprise with the basics, and Harlan had bought her the giant stuffed panda that sat in the corner by the window. In just under two weeks, her baby would be in that crib. Well, for the first couple of months in the bassinet that Harlan had commissioned for her, another surprise. She stared at the beautiful hand-carved rocking piece, imagining lifting Micah out to change him or to nurse in the glider chair, a lullaby playing softly. When she thought of the very near future like that, she felt so happy.

But then she'd be gripped by fear.

Like right now.

About being alone. No partner. No father. Just her.

You're going to be okay, she told herself. Stop whining and worrying. You're a doer. You've handled lots of sticky situations. You'll not only be okay, you'll be great at motherhood.

She let out a deep breath.

She did have the world's best mother and grandmother to help, and they were both full of experience. Her mom had already booked off from work the first week after Lily's due date.

It wasn't being a single mother in and of itself that had Lily so emotional. It was the longing for someone to be by her side through something so momentous, magical. Someone there. To share in parenting Micah. To love him the way she did. To love her.

Her mom and grandmother kept talking about joining an online dating site, but when she thought about what she was looking for in a man, she understood that he didn't exist. That she'd never get all that in one person.

A man like Gavin.

Yeah, Lily. Like Gavin but without the anvil on

his chest about his father. A heavy weight that had kept him from settling down. She couldn't count on him to stick around.

He wasn't the man for her and she had to stop fantasizing that he was.

The doorbell rang and Lily was glad for the interruption.

Gavin stood in the doorway, looking so gorgeous in jeans and a long-sleeved dark blue shirt rolled up to his forearms, Buddy beside him. Gavin had something in his hand, a piece of paper.

"Got a minute?" he asked her. "Something's come up."

"Sure."

He handed her the white paper.

LOST DOG. Arlo. Black-and-white border collie mix. Someone said they mighta seen him around the house.
Bill in the old cabin.

"Bill had a border collie?" she said, tilting her head. "Last I knew, he had a white shepherd mix named Snowy."

"Who's this Bill? He lives on the property?"

"Bill Pearson. He's in his eighties and used to help out in the cafeteria and do odd jobs. He once saved a ranch hand's life, and Harlan gave him use of a small old cabin, set back in the woods a bit, for life, as he put it. Handshake kind of thing. The guy whose life he saved brings him food every couple of weeks, checks in on him. Bill's always been very independent. Content to just have his cabin and his bookshelves full of Westerns. Never without a book in his hand."

"I guess I'll be bringing Buddy—Arlo—back to him, then," he said. If Lily wasn't seeing things, Gavin looked a bit sad about that.

"You've gotten attached to Buddy, huh?" she said.

"Eh, maybe a little." He knelt beside the collie and gave him a rub. "I can't keep a dog. I know that."

But you did get attached. Such a good sign. If he could get attached to a dog he thought was a stray, he could get attached to the Wild Canyon.

Maybe even to me.

There you go again, she thought. *Having useless fantasies.*

"I'll come with you," she said. "I know where the cabin is. It's pretty far out—five or so miles. He must not have had Buddy long if no one mentioned that the dog we found was Bill's. He has a cell phone, but he won't answer it. I tried to talk him into it last time I saw him, but he just waved his hand. He said he'd only use it for an emergency. He's a real old-school type."

"And eightysomething."

"Well, my gram is seventysomething and can probably bench-press Bill's weight and is a whiz at her cell phone and laptop."

He smiled. "Based on my visit to the caf, I'm not surprised to hear that." He glanced out the window. "It's dark out, and since we can't alert him we're coming, maybe we'd better wait till morning."

"Good idea," she said. "You get one more night with Buddy that way."

He looked down at the dog, who looked up at him.

You did get attached, she thought again.

There really is hope.

That strange sensation pulled at her belly again, and her hands flew to her stomach.

Gavin stepped closer, his hand steady on her shoulder. "You okay, Lily? Is something wrong? Should I call your mom?"

"I think I just need to sit down," she said.

He helped her over to the couch, Buddy sitting at her feet.

She sucked in a few breaths. "I had one of those weird pulling sensations again. But it's gone now. I can forget about trying to get up, though. Too bad because I have a wild craving for the chicken potpie my gram made me even though I had pizza not too long ago."

He sat down next to her. "Then you're lucky I'm around." He shot up. "I'll heat it up."

Of course he would. "Only if you have some too. You can't miss it."

"A forkful," he said. "Your mom and grandmother made sure I was well fed at the caf."

Lily smiled and watched him walk off into the kitchen. For just a moment she relished in the thought of her husband taking care of her, making sure her craving was satisfied, preparing dinner, bringing it all over to the coffee table.

I'm losing it, Buddy, she said silently to the dog. *Or maybe Arlo. No matter what your name is, you're a great dog. I'll slip you a little chicken, okay?*

The dog tilted his head. She'd miss the sweet guy if he lived way out with Bill. She'd also gotten attached. To Buddy and the man who'd found him and taken him in, cleaned him up, fed him and gave him belly rubs. A man who'd make a great husband. A great father. That she knew despite the fact that Gavin had been in her life such a short time.

He brought over a glass of ginger ale and a small plate of saltines.

She laughed. "How'd you know?" she asked, then munched on a cracker.

"I think everyone knows about the restorative powers of ginger ale and saltines, even if your bellyache isn't that kind of bellyache. I could come up with a better appetizer, though."

"Nah, I just want that potpie. Wait till you taste it. Nothing like it."

"If it's half as a good as the chili I had in the cafeteria, I believe you." He sat down on the far end of the sofa. Too far. "Fifteen minutes till dinner. So Bill Pearson helped out your mom and grandmother?"

"Not in years," she said. "Maybe until five years ago. He'd sit on a chair and chop vegetables, peel potatoes, that kind of thing, his book open beside him. Never nicked a knuckle, surprisingly. And surprisingly fast with a potato peeler too."

"I have to say, I've come to care about Buddy. If this Bill can't take care of him…"

"We'll see," she said, her heart practically bursting. "He's a good person. But Buddy was likely an outdoor dog."

"Can't imagine you sleeping on the cold, hard ground and not the memory foam pet bed I bought you," he said to the dog.

Lily laughed. Bought and overnighted to the ranch. But she sobered up pretty fast. Yes, he was attached to Buddy. But if Bill proved he could take care of the dog and wasn't neglectful of him, Gavin would give him back. Just like he'd leave after the promised period of time was up.

There was no way she wouldn't be head over belly in love with the man by week's end, let alone in eight weeks.

As the delicious aroma of the potpie filled the air, Gavin patted his rock-hard stomach with a "that smells amazing." Lily stared, once again surprised she could notice anything but how increasingly uncomfortable she felt physically. Maybe she just found Gavin that attractive. To the point that he distracted her from her own very pregnant state.

For the next twenty minutes they talked about their favorite foods. His was pizza and had been since he was a kid, particularly from the old-fashioned pizzeria that had been in business for over fifty years and always had a line. Lily had lost her taste for some of her former favorites, like cheeseburgers, surprisingly enough, and now constantly craved pistachio nuts and potato chips. Finally the oven timer dinged and Gavin got up, refusing Lily's offer to help, not that she could imagine getting up since the sofa was so plush—great for sinking in but not emerging from when very heavily pregnant.

He brought over their plates and they dug in,

Gavin agreeing it was the best potpie he'd ever had. Mmm, Lily thought. Even through a yawn, despite her two naps today, she savored the comforting dish, the potatoes and carrots so soft and delicately spiced. She was telling him a funny story about her father when Lily felt herself drifting off.

She snapped awake, startling, her eyes popping open. "I didn't just fall asleep sitting up while you were telling me something interesting, did I?"

"Actually you fell asleep in the middle of your own sentence about how your dad had to bake three kinds of cookies for your elementary school bake sale because your mother just had an emergency root canal, and he either burned a batch or added an extra cup of sugar and had to make—" He grinned. "That's when you fell asleep. I didn't get to hear what he had to make."

"I miss my dad so much," she said, wrapping her arms around her best she could. Everyone thought she looked so much like her mom and gram because she had their coloring, but she had her dad's face and expressions. "He had to make ten dozen cookies just to get enough of the three kinds we'd promised. He spent hours with me in the kitchen that day, telling me to do the opposite of everything he did when it came to baking."

"Sounds like a great dad. Really there for you and kind."

"Yeah. That was him. I could always count on him. It's how I know you'll be a great dad," she said without thinking, feeling her cheeks burn. She glanced away.

"I'm not going to be a dad," he said, abruptly standing and picking up their plates, his empty, hers with half her slice remaining. She could barely finish a meal these days—or remember to stop blurting stuff out that made Gavin Dawson retreat. That was the last thing she wanted.

He brought the plates to the kitchen, then came back and sat beside her.

She had to remember what he'd just said. No matter how great a dad he'd be, and he'd be amazing, she knew it, Gavin wasn't going to be Micah's father. That wasn't going to happen.

Still, she was glad she'd said it. Being emotionally honest was important to her. If you didn't say what was on your mind, what you believed and thought and felt, how did you have a real conversation?

"Want to know what a dope I am?" she said. "The weekend I spent with John—he's the guy who took off on me—I actually thought, this guy will make a great dad someday." She shook her head. "So what do I know about anything? I don't know why I think I can trust my own judgment."

"Hey," he said, his voice so gentle that tears stung

her eyes. "Everyone's been hurt or betrayed. Everyone at some point or another. Maybe that weekend,
John was just living in the moment. In thrall with
the woman he'd met. Yeah, he walked away. But it
doesn't necessarily mean the weekend was a lie."

Huh. Lily hadn't thought of it that way. Not
once, even after all the time she'd spent talking
about her baby's father, that weekend, the ghost-
ing, with Brianna and her mom and grandmother.
No one had put it quite that way.

She bit her lip. "I usually think I'm pretty smart.
That I can read a person a half mile away. The two
of us had instant chemistry, a real connection, so
much to talk about. So I let myself go with it. I
remember thinking, Lily, stop thinking so much
and just feel. I'd never slept with a guy I just met.
Never. But after the rodeo, then dinner at the romantic Italian restaurant in Brewster followed by
a moonlit walk along the river, I went back to his
hotel and we didn't leave for two days. Then when
I woke up the final morning, he was gone. The gal
at reception told me he checked out and paid for
the room before dawn."

"Doesn't mean you weren't special to him, if
just for those days, Lily. Or that the weekend didn't
matter. You're not exactly forgettable."

Okay, now tears were stinging her eyes. She
blinked them back.

"You always make me think of things a different way," she whispered.

"Same here," he said. "Or I wouldn't even be on this ranch, now would I?"

Oh, Gavin, she thought again with that same inward wistful, dreamy sigh.

"He doesn't know what he's about to miss," Gavin added, then seemed to freeze as if he'd said something that shocked him.

"I think Harlan knew what he missed out on," she said. "I could hear it in his voice when he told me he had a son in town. I could see it on his face. He was haunted by it, Gavin."

Gavin leaned his head against the cushion, the strain back on his face. "When I was staying with my cousins at their guest ranch, I'd look at all their kids—and there are six Dawsons and they all have children—and I'd try to imagine any of them turning their backs on those little people. It's really impossible. You'd have to be either made of stone or nothing."

"Harlan definitely wasn't made of nothing," she said gently. "His life until the point your mother made that call clearly did a number on him. We know a little why. Maybe he never got over the fact that he was abandoned on a doorstep. Maybe he wanted nothing to do with family life because of that and how he was raised—which we know nothing about."

Like how your past has done a number on you, she thought but didn't say. *And you're definitely not made of nothing either.* But stone was very difficult to chip away at.

Despite her focus on him, on them, another yawn escaped her.

"Well," he said quickly. "Someone's ready for bed is what I think."

She'd gone too far. Said too much. And now he was going to leave when she wanted him to stay. Even just a little longer. But she yawned again, barely able to keep her eyes open. "Maybe I'll just stretch out for a minute," she said.

Gavin reached out a hand to pull her up so she could go to bed.

But she stayed put, not wanting this night to end. *Don't leave.*

Now, why can't I say that out loud if it's what I'm thinking? I supposedly want a real conversation, don't I?

But she couldn't. It would mean putting him on the spot when he clearly needed some space. And revealing a little too much of herself.

That she needed him.

That snapped her awake again, her eyes opening. She did need him.

That was scary. Too scary to think about.

She yawned again, her body's need for sleep overtaking her brain—a good thing.

She shifted so that she was lying down, her head on the plush side pillow, her legs stretched out in front of her.

Ahhh, this was comfortable. She was all belly, as her gram put it, so she fit comfortably on the sofa, her belly reaching high in the air.

"I was thinking I'd stick around just in case you have another one of those pulling sensations and need to get to your doctor," Gavin said.

"Why are you so wonderful?" she whispered, her eyes drifting closed. *So wonderful. So gorgeous. So everything I want in a life partner.*

And a father for my child.

She was vaguely aware of him putting the chenille throw over her. She opened her eyes and reached her hands to his face and gently pulled him down to kiss him.

His lips were soft and hard at the same time. Now his hands were on her face as he deepened the kiss. She closed her eyes, every cell in her body tingling. If she wanted to meet her baby a few days early, all she had to do was keep this up.

But she was so comforted, so oddly comfortable, that she felt the pull of sleep, her closed eyes heavy, Gavin's face so clear in her mind it was as if she were looking at him.

At least he's staying here tonight, she thought happily as she felt herself drifting into sleep.

But not for good.

Gavin woke up in the middle of the night, stretched out on the love seat across from the sofa, where Lily was still sleeping, the throw he'd settled half around her tangled underneath her. His legs were hanging over the side of the love seat and there was just no way to get comfortable anymore, so he sat up, thinking he'd just crash on the thick-pile area rug, a pillow under his head.

That kiss. Once again, it had happened so naturally, them both moving toward each other's lips at the same time, and he'd wanted to kiss her so much that he hadn't reminded himself that being so attracted, so drawn to Lily Gold on all levels made no sense.

But he was drawn to her. Undeniably.

Was he just feeling very protective of her? That had to be it. He knew she was worried, despite his promise not to make any decisions about the ranch for eight weeks, for her future. Whether she'd have a job to come back to, a home to raise her baby in.

He didn't know what he'd be doing in eight weeks. Selling. Not selling.

And she'd just opened up to him about her child's father. He and Lily had been just…feeling close in that moment. That had to have been it.

Getting involved with Lily romantically was something he couldn't do. He'd never forgive himself if he hurt her. And he was heading in that direction if he kept going for her lips.

I'm not going to be a dad…

The way he saw it, the way he'd always seen it, was that he wouldn't know the first thing about being a father. He'd never had one. Failing in the most basic of responsibilities was in his genes, his DNA, his blood. If the man who'd helped bring him into the world could turn his back on the mother of his child, on him, then Gavin could do it. Traits were inherited. Gavin couldn't see ever doing what Harlan had; he couldn't imagine himself capable of such a terrible thing. But the possibility, because his own father had, had always lurked in the back of his mind. Fatherhood was a big blank for him.

It had cost him relationships over the years. Two girlfriends whom he'd cared for in particular had run for the hills when he'd told them he didn't want to be a father and wouldn't change his mind, so if that was a deal breaker… It had been. Then his most recent ex had cheated on him when he'd truly believed they had something really special.

He'd stopped dating after that, done with it all. All he could think back then was, What the hell was the point?

Now he couldn't stop thinking about a woman who was about to have a baby any day. A woman who'd just shared how she'd been left, how awful she'd felt.

He wouldn't hurt her. Which meant keeping his lips and hands to himself.

"Maz," Lily said suddenly.

He looked at her, but she was still sleeping.

"Maz," she said again, slightly turning, her eyes closed. "Maz. Lamaze."

Lamaze, he realized she was saying. He vaguely knew what it was, a class pregnant women took to prepare for childbirth. He was pretty sure. Breathing techniques.

Her face seemed tense, like whatever she was dreaming about wasn't making her happy.

He looked at her pretty blond hair in its low ponytail, her belly covered by the chenille throw, her chest rising up and down in sleep. The spray of eyelashes against her cheek.

I want you to be happy, Lily Gold. I want you to have everything you need, everything you want.

But if she was looking for a father for her baby, as her family made clear was something vital for her, that having a partner was important to her,

Get ready to relax and indulge with your **FREE BOOKS** and more!

Claim up to FOUR NEW BOOKS & TWO MYSTERY GIFTS – absolutely FREE!

Dear Reader,

We both know life can be difficult at times. That's why it's important to treat yourself so you can relax and recharge once in a while.

And I'd like to help you do this by sending you this amazing offer of up to FOUR brand new full length FREE BOOKS that WE pay for.

This is everything I have ready to send to you right now:

Try **Harlequin® Special Edition** books featuring comfort and strength in the support of loved ones and enjoying the journey no matter what life throws your way.

Try **Harlequin® Heartwarming™ Larger-Print** books featuring uplifting stories where the bonds of friendship, family and community unite.

Or **TRY BOTH!**

All we ask in return is that you answer 4 simple questions on the attached Treat Yourself survey. You'll get **Two Free Books** and **Two Mystery Gifts** from each series you try, *altogether worth over $20!* Who could pass up a deal like that?

Sincerely,

Pam Powers

Harlequin Reader Service

Treat Yourself to Free Books and Free Gifts.

Answer 4 fun questions and get rewarded.

► DETACH AND MAIL CARD TODAY! ►

	YES	NO
1. I LOVE reading a good book.		
2. I indulge and "treat" myself often.		
3. I love getting FREE things.		
4. Reading is one of my favorite activities.		

TREAT YOURSELF • Pick your 2 Free Books...

Yes! Please send me my Free Books from each series I select and Free Mystery Gifts. I understand that I am under no obligation to buy anything, as explained on the back of this card.

Which do you prefer?

❑ **Harlequin® Special Edition** 235/335 HDL GRCC
❑ **Harlequin® Heartwarming™ Larger-Print** 161/361 HDL GRCC
❑ **Try Both** 235/335 & 161/361 HDL GRCN

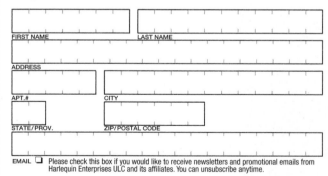

FIRST NAME

LAST NAME

ADDRESS

APT.#

CITY

STATE/PROV.

ZIP/POSTAL CODE

EMAIL ❑ Please check this box if you would like to receive newsletters and promotional emails from Harlequin Enterprises ULC and its affiliates. You can unsubscribe anytime.

© 2022 HARLEQUIN ENTERPRISES ULC
™ and ® are trademarks owned by Harlequin Enterprises ULC. Printed in the U.S.A.

SE/HW-820-TY22

then he'd have to step back. He had to do more than not kiss her. He had to put all thoughts of her as a woman out of his head.

Just think of her as your administrative assistant, he told himself. Boss. Employee. A drawn line.

But he'd already crossed it. He was getting way too close to her. Thinking of her way too much. Wanting to kiss her again when that made absolutely no sense, given where they each were in life.

So what the hell did he do?

Stepping back really wasn't an option; he cared about Lily. He did want to make her happy. But fatherhood wasn't in his future, let alone his immediate future. Neither was necessarily sticking around Bear Ridge—or keeping the Wild Canyon.

He'd have to figure out a plan, which was what he did—planned, plotted, executed a solid set of goals. He looked over at Buddy—Arlo, dammit—who peeled open an eye and tilted his head.

What am I gonna do here, Buddy? My entire life is upside down.

Buddy padded over and put his head just above Gavin's knee.

He could barely imagine giving this precious dog back to his rightful owner. How was he ever going to walk away from Lily Gold?

Chapter Nine

When Lily woke up on the sofa, a bit disoriented, Gavin was still there, as he said he would be, stretched out on the rug, his arm under his head and Buddy lying beside him.

Oh, Gavin, she thought for the hundredth time. And then she remembered the kiss. All they'd said. How he'd told her was staying over for the night just in case.

She closed her eyes and could still feel him leaning close, the press of his mouth to hers, the passion, even if the kiss lasted, like, five seconds. She could feel it.

If he wants to kiss you when you're nine months

*pregnant and falling asleep midsentence and are
expecting a baby any minute when the entire con-
cept of fatherhood doesn't work for him...*

She smiled and pulled herself to a sitting position, running her hands through her hair and
quickly working it into a loose braid down her
shoulder. Gavin Dawson had feelings for her. Her
heart gave another happy leap. She hadn't considered such a possibility when she'd been working
on her big plan to get him to love the ranch so he
wouldn't sell it.

That he could love her had never occurred to
her. But he was Gavin Dawson—special, wonderful—and that he'd fallen for a very pregnant single
woman shouldn't be such a surprise.

Neither would be his fight against his feelings.
He might care about her. But he didn't want to be
a father. And she was a package deal.

Remember that, Lily, she told herself. *He might
like the ranch. He might like you. But that doesn't
mean bubkes, as Dad used to say.*

"Morning," a deep male voice said.

She glanced over at Gavin to find him shooting up to his feet, giving the dog a pat. "Need
some help?"

She grinned. "I really do. It's how I know the
baby is probably gonna be early. I used to be able

to get myself off the sofa. Now, forget it. Gravity is at work."

He smiled and came over, reaching out both hands to take hers. His hands were so warm and strong. He gently pulled her up, and for a moment they were very close, her belly just about touching him.

"How are we also in kissing distance?" he asked.

"Must be something about us," she said almost on a whisper.

He gave one of her hands a squeeze, then stepped back. "I can imagine how excited you must be. To meet Micah."

She inwardly sighed, both at his discomfort about the kiss that he clearly didn't want to talk about and his gift at changing the subject to something that made her remember what really mattered. "Very. And a little nervous. I just want to do everything right."

"You will. You're Lily Gold."

She laughed. "Lily Gold has made plenty of mistakes."

"Caring so much is probably three-quarters of being a great parent," he said. "When people care about something, they make it work, make it happen, do what needs to be done."

"Yeah, I know you're right." *Of course I could*

say the same about you—and being a father. What-ever had led Harlan to make certain choices didn't mean Gavin would make those choices. "Give me a half hour," she added, needing a little break from this man who had her all turned around, "and we'll go see Bill Pearson."

"At the old cabin," he said with a nod and then a glance at Buddy. "I'll meet you on your porch in thirty. You'll be all right here on your own?"

"Got my trusty phone. You're a text away."

He nodded again.

She noticed he didn't seem remotely bothered that he'd be the first person she'd text if she did need help. But then again, he was the closest. Her mom and gram wouldn't be at the caf yet.

Two kisses. The first person she'd call.

This was all adding up to so much trouble. Without meaning to, he was making himself in-dispensable to her. It was supposed to be the other way around. The perfect admin to the new owner, showing him how great the ranch he'd inherited was. Making him want to stay. Granted, he clearly did have feelings for her, but that wouldn't neces-sarily make him stay. He was a man who left; that was how he lived his life.

The dog followed him out, and the moment the door closed, she wished he were back.

She managed to take a short shower with the

fancy handheld showerhead and hold bar her mother had installed, then put on a little makeup and dried her hair, going for her usual low ponytail to keep it out of her face. Maybe she'd cut it when Micah reached grabbing age. That probably wasn't too far off.

She slipped on her easiest outfit—a stretchy pale pink maternity dress—and put on a long heather-purple cardigan. She was out the door and on the porch with two minutes to spare.

And suddenly there was Gavin, his hair slightly damp, Buddy beside him.

She wondered if they'd return with the sweet, lovable dog. She really had no idea how this would go.

With Buddy in the cargo area of his SUV, Gavin pulled out and headed down the two-lane gravel road that led out to the main ranch. The big red barn came into view, with its wrought iron weather vane, the path to the animal sanctuary across from it. The two llamas were arriving tomorrow at twelve thirty, and the entire sanctuary team would be there to greet them and get them settled. Maybe with Jonah and Aria working so closely from here on in, one of them would finally ask the other out and put each other out of their love misery.

She smiled as she thought about asking Gavin

out. Last night had felt like a date. Being with Gavin in any capacity just felt...special.

"This place is so well-run," Gavin said, looking out the windshield. "I've consulted at ranches where you wouldn't see a soul, then a cow would amble by. Here, everyone I see looks purposeful, walking with direction. I can see a good number of hands in the fields and up on the outer ledges with the cattle. And the ranch is spotless."

"Harlan liked tidy," she said. "He insisted on it. Nothing out of place, nothing broken."

He gave a nod but didn't say anything.

"Make a left here, and the cabin will be about four miles up. There's a short path to get to it. It's pretty wooded. And probably why no one knew he'd taken in a dog. You can't even see the cabin from the road."

"Hard way of life for an eightysomething," Gavin said, glancing at her. "You said he's checked on often?"

"Yup. Daniel McJones—he's the ranch hand whose life Bill saved years ago—stops by often with groceries and takes Bill to the library. Like I said, Bill likes his Westerns. But he's never been very interested in people. Even when he helped out at the caf, he was pretty quiet. My mom and gram adored him. For a good few months after he retired from the caf, they'd stop by too, but he made it clear he didn't like visitors and just wanted to be on his own with his pup and his books and his woods."

"The hermit type," he said. "I don't often run into loners to that degree. I think of myself as a loner, but give me the woods and a cabin for more than two days, even with a dog and a good book, I'd go out of my mind."

You don't say... Lily's heart gave a little leap. Another good sign that Gavin Dawson was semi-ripe for the picking. She just had to wait until he was ready. Until he loved the Wild Canyon as she did.

Maybe...until he loved her. If that was even possible given how he felt about fatherhood.

"I wouldn't last half a day all alone," she said. "I like some time to myself but not more than a few hours. I need people around me. And soon enough," she added with a hand on her belly, "I'll have a little housemate." She sat up a bit straighter. "Ooh, there's the path. You can pull up right here. It's a very short walk but it's hidden."

Gavin helped her out, and they went to the back of the SUV to let out Buddy. Who was very likely Arlo. No matter what, he'd always be Buddy to her. Buddy was wagging his tail, glancing expectantly at them, like he was saying, *Let me out. I got someone to go see.*

Of course, he could have run back to the cabin at any time. He definitely liked the food at the main house. And the memory foam pet bed.

Once out of the vehicle, Buddy ran ahead up the path.

"Yeah, that's Arlo," he said, slightly grimacing. "He knows exactly where he's going."

"Well, let's go talk to Bill and see what the deal is."

They walked barely three minutes into the woods when the cabin appeared. Small and one story, made of the usual logs with a bright red door to help see it in heavy snowfall. The wood-shed close to the cabin was half-full. The area was so peaceful, with just the chirping of spring birds and the scent of the land.

Buddy gave a bark and the door opened. Out stepped Bill Pearson. In his mid or even late eighties, Bill was tall and thin and wearing his standard uniform: baggy blue jeans, a striped button-down shirt with a leather vest over it, cowboy hat and boots.

"You brought Arlo back. I appreciate it," he said, glancing from Lily to Gavin and then focusing on the dog. "Haven't had him long. I found him in the woods just a week ago. No idea where he came from."

"How'd you get all the way out to the main house to leave a note?" Lily asked.

"I asked Daniel to give me a ride there and back. I don't hold it over his head that I saved his life, but he says yes to any favors I ask. 'Course, I don't often."

"Bill, this is Gavin Dawson. He inherited the ranch when Harlan passed. Gavin, Bill Pearson."

Bill stepped forward, his gaze laser focused on Gavin. "Whatcha gonna do with the place?" he asked.

"Million-dollar question," Gavin said. "I really don't know yet. I understand that Harlan gave you the cabin for life for saving Daniel's life. I'll honor that, of course."

"Unless you sell," Bill said. "Then I'm out on my caboose."

"Well, Gavin's not making any decisions for at least eight weeks," Lily said.

"This is a grand place," Bill said. "I worked a lot of ranches in my time but none as grand as this."

"It is a special place," Lily said. "I'm sorry that we didn't realize Buddy—Arlo—was your dog, Bill. You must have missed him."

"Now it's my turn to be honest," Bill said. "I'm not really up to caring for a scrappy young dog. I just figured if I left a note, you'd bring him over and I could size you up, find out if you were okay with taking him in. He's a good boy."

"He is," Gavin said. "From your note, I thought you wanted him back."

"Well, I do," Bill said, reaching a hand down to pet Buddy. "But I can't do right by him alone at my age. I'll be eighty-eight soon."

"I'll take good care of him," Gavin said. "That I can absolutely promise."

Lily could feel Gavin's relief. His shoulders had relaxed some, and the hard line of his jaw softened just a bit.

Bill's face lit up. "I'm real happy to hear that."

"When's your big day, Bill?" Lily asked. "We'll bring over a cake and sing you happy birthday."

Bill waved a hand in the air. "I don't bother celebrating stuff like that. I'll just take a walk in the woods, see what leaves and trees and berries I can identify." Bill let out a yawn. "Well, time for my nap. Thank you for coming by." He looked down at Buddy. "You come visit whenever you want, you hear?"

Buddy tilted his head at Bill and got another pat, then Bill headed back inside.

"Well," Gavin said. "I guess I have myself a dog."

"You definitely do."

Just like you have a home, she wanted to say. *A home and now a dog*.

Gavin knelt down. "You want to come home with us?" he asked. "Well, with me," he added quickly. "But Lily is very close. Right next door."

Buddy wagged his tail.

As Gavin stood, he said, "I guess Bill's all right out here. He seems in good shape, mentally, physically. Knows who he is, for sure."

"Yup, that's Bill."

"There's something familiar about him," Gavin said. "He reminds me of someone, but I can't put my finger on it."

"Well, no one looks quite like Bill, with his leather vest and Stetson," she said with a smile. "If you'd met him, you'd remember."

"No doubt." He looked down at Buddy. "You ready to head home?" he asked.

More tail wagging.

It didn't escape Lily that twice now Gavin referred to the house as home.

Once the two llamas were settled in their new home, their pretty new pasture to the right of the goats', Gavin stood with Lily on the other side of the wood fence, watching them. They weren't doing much. Jonah and Aria were inside their pen in the barn, spreading out the hay for their bedding.

"They're kind of cute," Gavin said, looking at the whitish one with its smushed-in face. "He has to be over five feet tall."

"Five foot four, to be exact. Same as me. And his friend is five-five. They're both male. Llamas are very sweet but they don't love to be handled too much."

"Kind but they like their space. Like Bill Pearson." He thought of the elderly man in his baggy jeans and leather vest, his sharp green eyes. Quite a character. Big ranches were full of them. Gavin had met his share.

She smiled. "Exactly." Her phone dinged and she pulled it from her pocket. "My own chiming reminder about my last Lamaze class today at six. Maybe I'll skip it."

"You were saying Lamaze in your sleep last night."

"What? I was not."

He nodded on a smile, last night flashing through his mind. The potpie. Lily on the sofa. The kiss. "Yup. You said maz a couple times. Then Lamaze. Maybe you were dreaming of the class."

"Doubt it. It's okay, I guess. But the schedule changed to my mom and gram's busy hours at the caf, so I go alone. My good friend Brianna has come with me a couple of times, but she has little kids and can't usually make it."

"I'll go with you tonight," he said—once again, for the hundredth time when it came to Lily Gold—without thinking first.

Her eyes widened. "Really?"

"Sure," he said. "It's about breathing, right? Practicing for the big day. I can help you do that."

She stared at him. "You won't be uncomfortable? It's a bunch of pregnant women and their partners. Mostly husbands."

"I'll be uncomfortablish," he said. "But that's my life now, isn't it?" Understatement.

"But you kind of have to be here at the Wild Canyon," she said. "You don't have to be at my Lamaze class."

How did he explain—without actually saying so—that he wanted to be there for her? That it was her last class, that it was important and probably meaningful, to the point that for whatever reason, she was talking about it in her sleep? Which he knew because he'd been right there, unwilling to leave her alone when she'd had that one strange sensation.

"I want to go for you," he heard himself say.

The sweet, surprised smile he just got made it even more worth it. "To be honest, I'm really glad you offered. I hate going alone. I always feel judged, even though no one probably even notices I'm there on my own or with my mom. I just feel so alone there."

"Well, tonight you won't feel that way."

I don't want you to feel like that ever.

"Did you know that llamas can live till twenty?" Jonah asked, coming out of the small barn where the llamas had their pen. "Aria just told me that. We're finished laying the bedding."

"These two are around twelve or so," Lily said. "According to the vet." She glanced around. "Is Aria done in the barn?"

"Just putting something away," he said, looking at his feet.

Aria came out and Gavin smiled at how similarly she and Jonah were dressed. Cowboy hats. Long-sleeved Henleys. Jeans. Boots. The outfit of a ranch hand. Aria stood beside Lily, looking at the llamas, and Jonah moved to the far side, next to Gavin.

Jonah, Jonah, Jonah.

Gavin could feel Aria's disappointment without the young woman saying a word. It was all on her face.

Jonah hadn't been able to get out of the pen fast enough. But he was so caught up in his own head, tongue-tied around her, that he couldn't seem to handle actually being near her.

Maybe Gavin would play matchmaker. Invite him and Aria—and Lily—over to dinner in the guise of a work meeting to discuss the sanctuary, something casual, like a barbecue. Just something to get the young couple started. The kid who'd squirmed in his office the other day needed a kick in the pants, and Gavin had just the foot.

Jonah had gotten under his skin. The kid was honest, and Gavin liked honest. He also saw the heart in Jonah, the potential. He was very young.

Lamaze partner. Matchmaker.

Who was Gavin becoming?

His phone rang. The lawyer—Harlan Mandeville's. Gavin had left Lamont Jones a voice mail this morning asking if Harlan had left any personal documents in the house or with the attorney. Gavin excused himself and walked a bit away.

"Thanks for calling back," Gavin said.

"There is a stipulation in the will," the attorney said. "Harlan did leave a file for you, an accordion folder with your name on it. The will stipulates that I not give it to you until five weeks after his death."

"Five weeks," Gavin repeated. "Why?"

"That I don't know," Lamont Jones said. He named the earliest date that Gavin could pick up the folder.

Gavin inwardly sighed. What was in that accordion folder? And did he actually want to know?

He shoved the phone back in his pocket and walked back over to the fence. *Put it out of your head until you can pick up the folder*, he told himself. *Just forget it right now.* To force the issue aside, he turned to Lily. "I'd like to invite the sanctuary team to a work dinner tomorrow night, if you're all free. Casual, some steaks on the grill. I'd like to get more up to speed on how we see the sanctuary going forward, how many animals we can safely take in, if we're focusing on recuperation or seniors, that kind of thing."

"I'll be there," Lily said. "Jonah, Aria, you're both free?"

"I am," Aria said brightly, tossing her long, dark braid behind her shoulder.

"Yeah, I can make it," Jonah finally said, his cheeks a bit flushed.

Lily was beaming. Pregnancy glow or had he just made her happy? Again.

She reached over and gave his hand a squeeze. He never wanted her to let go.

Lily noticed that Gavin was quiet on the way to Lamaze class, not so unusual for him, but maybe he was regretting having offered to come with her. His jawline seemed tight, his hands heavy on the wheel of his SUV. A man about to accompany a pregnant woman—whom he hadn't known two weeks ago—to childbirth class.

Maybe Gavin would join in, puffing out his breaths in quick succession to get through it with the least amount of pain.

She sneaked a glance at him. Yup. Strained. He looked at her and gave her a pleasant smile, one of those Gavin Dawson smiles that hid so much. But she'd begun to be able to read him.

He pulled up in front of the brick building that housed several wellness businesses, a family therapist, a massage therapist, an acupuncturist and the doula who taught the Lamaze class. The doula, recommended by Brianna, had been through childbirth four times, and Lily always looked forward to being in her calming presence these past weeks. Today was the final class, and Lily had no idea if she was ready for childbirth or not. Her plan involved deciding on an epidural in the moment since her OB had said she'd let Lily know when there was no turning back from going "natural."

It was so hard to make decisions about something she'd never experienced. Including feeling the way she did about Gavin. Taking a big step back or forward was impossible since she had no idea what was going to happen—if he'd leave. If he'd stay. If he'd stay and never kiss her again. She usually wouldn't like not being in control of her own head and heart, but she was trying to let her heart lead the way and not listen so much to her warnings.

Gavin got out of the SUV and opened her door for her, helping her down. "My first Lamaze class."

"Life is definitely full of surprises," Lily said as they entered the building. "You probably never thought you'd be walking into a childbirth class." But this was the man who'd invited her, Jonah and Aria to a barbecue at his house tomorrow night to talk sanctuary business. He didn't have to do that. There was really no reason for a whole dinner; they could have had a quick meeting earlier to go over where the sanctuary would go from here.

He'd arranged the dinner because he knew how much they all cared about the sanctuary. And maybe even because he'd picked up on the serious crush vibes between Jonah and Aria.

But accompanying her to Lamaze might be a step too far. Too much new too fast? Too much change? Too much being thrown at him? Suddenly she wondered if the class would be the tipping point that would send him out of Bear Ridge and back to his life on the road, on other people's ranches. Fixing their lives. Avoiding his own.

"Never did," he said, pressing the up elevator button.

She glanced at him, but for all anyone knew,

he was going to the gym to work out or to pick up takeout. Neutral expression. No hint of the earlier strain she'd seen while he'd been driving. He was here for her and Gavin Dawson wouldn't show his discomfort. That's who he was.

Class would start in about ten minutes, so they had some time to find their spot and get settled. For Gavin to push out his breaths.

Just as they were stepping into the elevator, his phone pinged with a text. He pulled it out of his pocket and read the screen, while Lily pushed the elevator button for the second floor.

"Wow, first Lamaze class," he said, "and now a reminder about my niece and nephew's double one-year-old birthday party at my cousins' dude ranch on Saturday afternoon. My tiny cousins once or twice removed or third cousins, not sure—but they're both turning one soon, so their parents are throwing a big party for them. I haven't been to a kiddie party since I was a kid."

"I've run into the Dawsons in town, and they're always surrounded by babies and toddlers. Lots of children among them. They always look so happy—even when a baby is shrieking."

He nodded. "All six of them have settled down and have kids. When I was staying at their guest ranch, I was constantly being overrun by strollers and toddlers, and that was just the Dawson bunch."

"Ooh, I'd love to go to a party like that. Talk about seeing babies and toddlers in action at all ages and stages." She felt her cheeks burn. "Not that I'm inviting myself."

"Actually, I'd really appreciate it if you'd come with me," he said. "Don't make me go alone. Please."

She laughed. "Well, good. Then it's a date. I mean, not a date, a—"

She shut up fast, thinking of their kiss last night—which they still hadn't talked about. And maybe there was no reason to. They both knew it had happened. No reason to dissect it, make decisions about their attraction they obviously couldn't deny. One kiss had turned into two now. And Lily wanted a third. This morning, that kiss was the first thing she thought about it. Followed by what it would be like to be with Gavin—once she had the baby and her body back.

Brianna had said sex had been the last thing on her mind even a few months after her second baby was born. But falling for a man at nine months pregnant had her fantasizing about lying naked with Gavin and exploring every inch of his body. She could see her attraction to him being so strong that the minute she was cleared for sex, she'd be all over him.

She could also see Brianna laughing in her face

at that one. Brianna had been madly in love with her husband since high school and they were the PDA king and queen of Bear Ridge.

She cleared her throat. "You know what I mean. An event. That we'll attend together." Now she was all tongue-tied around him? Maybe because she was thinking about sex when he was standing so close beside her in the small elevator.

The doors slid open. "Here we are," she said, pointing across the hall at the painted door with pastel stripes.

He smiled and pulled open the door and she couldn't get inside fast enough. She needed some of that calming vibe the pretty room and the earth mother instructor always lent her.

The large room was welcoming and inviting with blond wood floors and huge floor-to-ceiling windows covered by sheer white curtains. Ten big mats were set around the room. Lily smiled at the couples already there. Dylan and Jenna, married two years and expecting their first. They held hands through the entire class. Then there was Maggie Pfifer, who always stared at Lily when she came in, her gaze going to whomever she brought and then shooting back to Lily as if to say, *Aw, poor thing with no ring, had to bring your mom.* Maggie was one of the most perfect gazelle-type creatures with a matching husband and one of the rare people who for some reason pushed Lily's buttons and got to her. Without saying a word. Which meant it was Lily projecting onto the woman, who was probably not giving her a thought at all.

She thought she'd finally feel like one of the group with Gavin coming with her, but this was the final class and everyone knew she wasn't married and that the tall, good-looking guy with her wasn't her partner.

Just my boss, she wanted to shout out.

She frowned, realizing she was letting herself go places she shouldn't. *Just calm down, Lily.* She puffed out a couple of early breaths.

Gavin had a hand on her shoulder instantly. "You okay? Need to sit?"

"I'm fine, really," she said. "Just always feel... off here, even though the class itself is so helpful."

He squeezed her shoulder. "Yeah, I know that feeling."

She had no doubt of that. All the fighting he did in his own head and heart. She knew he liked the Wild Canyon—a lot—but he wouldn't let himself enjoy it. He barely seemed to look around the place, just kept his focus on whatever he was doing at the moment, like at the sanctuary to welcome the llamas this morning. He was still battling any feeling of home when it came to the Wild Canyon.

Again she thought about the dinner invitation

he'd issued to the sanctuary staff. That was definitely unusual. Gavin had spent some time with Jonah to go over the mentorship program, and given how direct and brutally honest Jonah could be sometimes, he likely said something that had tugged at Gavin's heartstrings, whether about Harlan or the ranch or Aria. All Lily knew was that he cared about Jonah enough to even think about arranging the little dinner party at his house. And if he cared about Jonah, that meant the ranch, the employees, were getting through.

The instructor, Vivienne, arrived, looking serene as usual, and Lily felt herself already getting into Lamaze mode. Gavin followed Vivienne's directions to move behind his partner and open his legs wide so that Lily could rest against him, practically upright.

The moment her back hit his chest, she almost froze, the intimacy of leaning against him that way, so physically close, almost too much to bear. She thought he'd be the one to freak out at childbirth class? Ha.

She could feel his heartbeat.

And hers was now thundering in her ears.

Breathe, Lily. One, two, three, four, five.

First a Lamaze class, now a double one-year-old birthday party. The two of them, again. Like they were a couple.

As the class got underway, Lily found herself much more aware of Gavin Dawson than of her own breaths. She closed her eyes, knowing that she was slipping past her own defenses and right into love and that there was nothing she could do about it.

Chapter Ten

To distract himself from Lily, from the Lamaze class and how off-balance he'd felt there earlier tonight—not that he'd let it show—Gavin had put in a few hours' work in his office, studying the books, going over reports from the foreman, reading employee records, immersing himself in all things Wild Canyon. He signed more invoices, answered at least twenty emails and responded to his cousin Daisy's text, saying that he would be at Tony and Chloe's double one-year birthday party and would be bringing a guest, if that was all right. Daisy typed back an of course. Tony was her son, and she was pregnant with her second baby.

There was a folder labeled Press in the desk drawer, and Gavin had read through it. Harlan Mandeville had started the ranch from nothing. He'd bought a patch of land, did some good work with breeding cattle and kept buying acreage and more cattle, and soon enough he had himself an empire. None of the articles mentioned where he'd come from, where he'd been born, who his parents had been.

He typed Harlan Mandeville, Brewster County into the search engine again. There were at least one hundred hits, all of which he'd scoured before, local news articles about the ranch or Wyoming magazine pieces on the Wild Canyon. There were two on the main houses and the stable's architecture, accompanied by glossy photos of the living room with the gorgeous woodwork, beams and the stone fireplace. Many of the hits were about cattle and horse sales. And then there was his obituary, which he could tell Lily had written. There was very little personal information. He was relieved to see she hadn't included something like "Harlan is survived by his son, Gavin Dawson."

That would have bothered him. He still didn't consider himself Harlan Mandeville's son; the man would had to have been his father, even a crappy one, for that. Harlan had fathered him was all. Then their connection stopped.

Why was Harlan's life such a mystery? What was his story? He'd been left on a doorstep, but whose house? Where? And what happened after that? Maybe he could call the local schools in the county and see if Harlan had been a student anywhere. That would give him the town where he'd been raised. Schools tended to keep those records for alumni purposes and class reunions. There had to be a photo of Harlan Mandeville, high school senior, in some yearbook.

If he'd been born and raised in Wyoming. It was possible he'd come from out of state. But again, Bear Ridge would be an odd choice out of the clear blue sky. He was from here, the area, that much Gavin would bet on.

He clicked out of the search engine. He'd had enough of Harlan Mandeville. He grabbed a pad and pen and started a list titled To Do.

Buy groceries for the work BBQ tomorrow night.
Buy presents for the double birthday party Saturday afternoon.
Maybe get Lily something.

Wasn't he supposed to be not thinking of her? Not buying her gifts?

Her beautiful face floated into his mind, her big blue eyes.

Her very pregnant belly.

He grabbed his phone and texted her.

Feeling okay? Need anything?

He waited, hoping she'd text back right away. When the little dots appeared and he knew she was typing, a flood of relief came over him. Connection to her. It had become that important to him. She had become that important.

Feeling just fine. Thank you. For everything today.

Always, he typed back.

But did he mean that? Always?

Lily couldn't have asked for nicer weather for the sanctuary barbecue in Gavin's backyard. There was a gorgeous April breeze, it was sixty-three degrees and the sun was still bright at seven fifteen. While Lily reclined on a padded chaise longue with a plastic tumbler of very refreshing herbal iced tea and her craving of the day—supersharp cheddar on the salty crackers Gavin had set out—he was at the grill, turning the chicken he'd brushed with a tangy mesquite sauce. She watched him flip the asparagus. And once again she was lost in a fantasy. That Gavin was her husband in this very cozy scene.

Jonah and Aria were throwing sticks for Buddy—Gavin had decided to keep that name and give him the middle name Arlo. Though Jonah would smile and laugh every now and then, he seemed strained, never getting too close to Aria. She'd step near him and he'd suddenly go looking for a stick to throw for Buddy. Aria had dressed up for the occasion in a sundress and flat sandals, and even Jonah had exchanged his usual long-sleeved T-shirt or Henley for a button-down shirt, sleeves rolled up.

You could lead a horse to water… she thought with a smile. Jonah was who he was, and he'd either come out of his shell where the young woman of his dreams was concerned or he wouldn't. Timing was always crucial. Maybe he just wasn't ready for Aria.

"Everything's ready," Gavin said, coming over to the big round patio table with his platter of chicken and asparagus. The table had been set, and there were three bowls—one with a tossed salad that Lily had put together, one with her mother's potato salad made fresh today at the caf and Aria's pesto pasta salad.

Gavin set the platter down and then pulled Lily up from her recliner.

"I can't wait until I can get up from a chair without help," she said with a smile.

"Does it hurt to be pregnant?" Aria asked as they sat around the table, her brown eyes curious. "I mean, right now, what does it feel like?"

"Doesn't hurt," Lily said. "I can feel Micah kicking or moving sometimes. Like right now, pow!" She laughed, rubbing her side where his foot had jabbed her.

"Amazing," Aria said. "I want five kids just like my parents have. I'm really close with my siblings, even the two that are, like, more than ten years older. I'm the youngest."

"You're lucky," Gavin said, using the tongs to take a piece of chicken. "My cousins who own the Dawson Family Guest Ranch in town—there are six of them and they're very close too. They're very lucky to have each other."

"Eh, doesn't mean anything," Jonah said from his seat beside Aria, facing Gavin. "My dad has brothers and they don't even talk to each other. And look at Harlan and Gavin. They didn't even know each other. Father and son."

"Jonah," Lily snapped.

"What?" Jonah said. "It's the truth."

Aria stared at him. "Doesn't mean you have

to bring it up." She passed the platter of chicken to him.

He took it, holding her gaze, and something seemed to shift in him. "Sorry," he said, then glanced at Gavin. "Sorry. I guess I just hate talking about family."

Aria reached over and covered his hand on the table with hers. "All families are different. Some are great, some suck, some are close, some are estranged. Some are in the middle. Yeah, I'm lucky with mine. But you have family here, Jonah. Harlan was your family. David is your family. Lily's your family. Felix and Dodie are your family, and now so are Charlie and Dumpling. Soon enough, I'm sure Gavin will feel like family."

"Yeah, if he doesn't sell the ranch," Jonah said, shooting a quick glance before sitting back.

"Why don't we eat," Lily said, handing Jonah Aria's bowl of pesto pasta.

Jonah took the bowl. "This looks really good," he said, heaping some on his plate.

Aria smiled. "I made it. Family recipe. It's so good."

Jonah took a bite. "It is."

She grinned and put some on her plate, then reached for the potato salad.

Soon they were busy eating and talking about

the food and the pair of goats and llamas, the earlier tension gone.

"Aw, even Buddy has his own plate," Aria said.

Gavin looked over at the dog, now stretched out on the deck in the sun. "I gave him some plain chicken. He gobbled it up in half a second."

"So what's the deal with Buddy?" Jonah asked. "He belonged to that old man in the hidden cabin, but he gave him to you?"

"Bill didn't have Buddy long," Gavin said. "He found him in the woods, but he's almost eighty-eight and was having trouble caring for him."

Jonah tilted his head. "But why post a lost-dog sign at the office if he didn't intend to keep Buddy?"

"Maybe just to be assured that Buddy was in good hands," Lily said. "Or maybe to meet Gavin, the new owner of the ranch. To be assured Bill could stay in the cabin."

Jonah took a sip of his iced tea. "I once asked Harlan why he let the old guy stay in the cabin, and he said he saved a cowboy's life and that made him a friend of the Wild Canyon for life. Free room and board for life. That's cool."

Lily smiled. "I'm glad because I don't think Bill has anywhere else to go."

Jonah grimaced. "That'll be me at eighty-eight. Living in old Bill Pearson's hidden cabin."

"Sorry," Gavin said with a smile. "You'll have to save someone's life for that."

Jonah tilted his head, his mop of brown hair falling to the side. "So you're not gonna sell the ranch?"

"Not making any decisions for at least eight weeks," Gavin said. "Till I get the lay of the land. Really understand the place."

"I hope you keep it," Aria said. "The Wild Canyon is special."

"Yeah, it is," Jonah agreed, looking at her.

"Speaking of the Wild Canyon, let's get to sanctuary business," Gavin said. "Lily, can you fill me in on where we are, how much room we have for additional animals, what type of animals we're taking, all that? I know the basics."

Lily was glad for the change of subject, especially on to something that all four of them had a special interest in, hence the dinner gathering in the first place. She went over the details, that they'd take any injured animals who had nowhere else to go and any senior animals who were past their prime for their ranches. Whether wild or from area farms.

"When I first heard about the animal sanctuary, I thought it was the craziest thing," Jonah said. "I mean, a cattle ranch isn't about pet cows. But Harlan explained it to me. He said every creature needs a place to go, someplace where someone will take care of them, from a snail to an elephant."

"That's really, really nice," Aria said. "To care that way."

"That's what I don't get, though," Jonah said. "He cares about snails and llamas but not his own kid?" His face turned a bit red and he shot a glance at Gavin. "He said he understood what it's like to be a throwaway but then just throws away the chance to know his son? Huh? I just don't get it."

"Hey," Gavin said. "I don't get it either. But what I've learned over the years is that people are complicated."

"I don't know," Jonah said. "What's complicated about taking care of your own kid?"

Lily looked at Gavin. His expression was half shut-this-guy-up and half compassion. Because it was clear that Jonah was talking about himself here.

"Children are a big deal," Gavin said. "Maybe Harlan was afraid he wasn't up to the job of being someone's father. That's an important title." He looked over at Lily and then quickly back to Jonah.

Was he trying to explain himself to her? The *I'm not going to be a dad*?

"I'm surprised to hear you defending him," Jonah said, pausing with his hand on the pesto pasta serving spoon.

Gavin paused too. "Yeah, me too. Though I wouldn't say it's a defense. More like me trying to understand. That's the key, really. Trying to see where people are coming from instead of standing in judgment." He froze—for just a second, Lily noticed, as if taking that in himself.

"I'm a big-time judger," Jonah said.

Gavin smiled. "I noticed."

Aria picked up her iced tea. "I'm not. I'm with Gavin. It's important to understand where people are coming from, why they act the way they do, do the things they do. Like my twin brother, Andrew. He worked so hard to get into a good college and thought he wanted to be a doctor. Now he's dropping out to join the Marines. My parents are proud and scared at the same time. But he told me he held on to that dream of becoming a doctor like a crutch when it long stopped being what he really wants to do. He wants to be a military medic."

"It's definitely not easy to let go of something you've held on to a long time," Lily said. "But when you do, when you really let go and focus on what you actually want, it's very freeing."

She could feel Gavin's eyes on her. Knew he was wondering exactly what she was talking about. They'd hit on it some two nights ago, when he'd been kind about her baby's father and his disappearance from her life.

It was some of that. Throughout her pregnancy she'd held on to the idea that her baby's father would come back, looking all over for her, having realized he'd made a huge mistake by just walking out on her. Of course, that had never happened. She'd never seen him again. It had taken a long time to let it all go.

But the fundamentals of that dream—the husband, the great dad for Micah—that she'd keep tight hold of. She did want family barbecues and photographs lining the stairs.

Gavin Dawson had stepped right into all that. Not like a white knight, though.

She would rescue herself, as she always did. If in eight weeks he chose to sell the Wild Canyon, chose to leave, she would go on, focusing on motherhood and the future. Not her heartbreak. But the dream of finding someone to share her life with? She'd hold on to that.

"Well, I don't know how to do that," Jonah said. "Everything I think and believe is because of the past twenty years. How I was raised, what my parents were like. I can't just pretend none of that happened and suddenly think life is all sunshine and animal sanctuaries."

"But maybe you don't let stuff you don't like from your past make decisions for your future," Aria said. "If that makes sense."

"But how can I stop doing that?" Jonah asked. "That's what I don't get."

"I hear you, Jonah," Gavin said. "Billion-dollar question. How do you just let it go?"

Lily looked from Gavin to Jonah, both deep in thought. Then she glanced at Aria, who looked hopeful.

Aria had the right idea. This was a start. More than a start, it was a push, a kick in the pants. These two hard heads were thinking. Dealing instead of burying and ignoring.

That was how you just let it go. In steps and stages.

But Lily couldn't imagine life without Gavin Dawson at this point. He'd become too special, too indispensable.

She'd fallen in love.

Two hours later, Gavin and Lily lay on side-by-side chaise longues, the cake Aria had brought from the great bakery in town between them, along with two cups of coffee, both decaf. The night air felt good on Gavin's face, the cool April breeze refreshing. The back porch light was on, and two light posts cast soft illumination on Lily's beautiful face. He was glad she hadn't left when Jonah and Aria had. The heavy conversation had left him a bit unsettled, and it was as if she'd instinctively known he wouldn't mind if she stuck around and debriefed him. She was good at that.

"You're so good with Jonah," she said, wrapping her long cardigan around her.

There it was. How Lily understood Gavin so well was a mystery to him, but he was glad she did. He did want to talk about Jonah and all that had come up.

"You think so?" he asked, turning to face her. "I try not to stare him down and tell him to mind his own business and to shut the hell up, but I'm afraid it comes through in my expression."

She laughed. "Nope. You're gentle with him. He needs everything you're doing, Gavin."

"I don't know how I know that, but I do. I hate to say something Harlan said, I hate it more than anything, but damn, that kid reminds me of me."

Lily smiled. "He's trying to find his way. Answers. To deal with all the gunk in his life. Really painful stuff. It's either cry or throw out some barbed zingers at other people. So that's what he's been doing. And you never focus on the zingers. You focus on what's behind them. I'm grateful for you, Gavin Dawson."

He stood up and walked to the edge of the patio, watching Buddy sniffing under a tree. "I don't know what the hell I'm doing."

"Help me up?" she asked, and he turned and

reached out both hands to get her to her feet. She didn't let go of one hand. "Maybe you don't know consciously. When it comes to your own stuff. But you're going to change Jonah's life, Gavin. I can feel it."

He stepped closer to her and then held out his arms and she fell right into them, her belly pressed against him. He could smell her flowery shampoo. Her head was against his chest and he leaned atop hers. Everything slipped away—what they'd been talking about, what he'd been thinking about. All he felt was Lily, holding her, being with her. And everything felt okay.

Lamaze class.

A barbecue that was supposed to be business and a little matchmaking had turned very personal.

And now tomorrow he was taking Lily to a family birthday party. A double one-year-old party. Babies. Children. Family.

He barely recognized himself here at the Wild Canyon.

Some days he thought that might be a good thing. Other times it seemed a good reason to leave in eight weeks.

She looked up, her beautiful lips so close. What he would give to kiss her—for the next five hours, have her share his bed, just so he could lie beside her, have her close.

She stepped away and he missed the feel of her in his arms. How was he going to leave when her maternity leave was up? He could sell the place to someone he trusted, but then he'd have no reason to stop in every few months to see Lily. See her baby. Check in.

Was that his plan? To leave and stop in? As if the woman standing by the deck railing was just some acquaintance?

He had no idea what his plan was. What he was going to do with the Wild Canyon.

Or with his feelings for Lily Gold.

Chapter Eleven

The double birthday party for the one-year-olds was being held in the huge backyard of the main house at the Dawson Family Guest Ranch. Gavin stood watching the crowd, a flavored seltzer in his hand, Lily beside him with a bottle of water. He'd tried pointing out whose kid was whose, but there were just too many Dawsons for that.

There were babies and toddlers everywhere Gavin looked, including one little boy—maybe three years old—who'd just crashed into his leg and bounced backward onto his bottom on the grass.

Gavin hurried over to the cute kid and knelt down. "Hey, are you okay?"

The boy grinned and shot up, flying a stuffed lion in a cape overhead, then went running off.

"Sorry!" said his cousin Axel, staring after the boy who was running through the crowd, another little boy joining him. "Danny is a sprinter."

"He's very cute," Gavin said.

Axel's wife, Sadie, came over holding their baby daughter. Gavin remembered meeting Sadie during the short time he'd been at the ranch, but he couldn't recall how old the baby was. Three or four months. There were just so many little Dawsons. Sadie turned to Lily. "Hi, I'm Sadie Dawson. You look so familiar—I've definitely seen you in town, but I don't think we've met."

Lily smiled. "Lily Gold. I'm the admin at the Wild Canyon."

"That's where I know you from," Axel said. "I've seen you at a few cattle auctions and rancher-association meetings."

Lily smiled. "Yup, I like to attend those kinds of events. Your baby girl is so beautiful. Three months?"

"Almost four," Sadie said, giving the baby a gentle rock. "If you need any recs for anything baby related, I'm your gal."

Lily grinned. "I can't believe my son will be

here in just over a week. I can't wait. I am so ready."

"Yup, that's how I felt when I was nine months," Sadie said.

More Dawsons with more babies came over, congratulating Lily on the big-day-to-be. Gavin's cousin Ford was holding his baby boy—West—as if he'd been a father forever. Granted, Gavin hadn't been too close with any of his Bear Ridge cousins, but he'd gotten to know some of them when they were growing up, and the week he'd spent at the ranch had brought him closer to all of them. Ford, the big-city cop turned Bear Ridge cop, was the last Dawson Gavin would have expected to settle down and start a family. But here he was, looking so proud and happy, his wife, Danica, chatting away with Lily.

A woman Gavin didn't recognize, a mom of one of the little guests, walked over with a baby in a chest carrier and joined the conversation with Lily and Danica. Then she turned to Gavin. "Will this be your first child?" she asked.

Gavin could feel his face burn.

He glanced at Lily, whose eyes widened.

"I'm not… I mean, we're not—" he started.

"Oh, I thought you were together. Sorry," she said before making a fast getaway.

Gavin stared at the baby in Ford's arms. Then

at another baby. And another. Then over at the toddlers running circles around one of the tables.

I'm not going to be a dad...

His chest felt tight and he slid a finger in the back of his collar. Was it suddenly twenty degrees hotter? As the group disbanded and mingled with others, Lily slid over to him.

"Sorry about that," she said. "You looked like you might faint or something."

"It's so hard for me to imagine being mistaken for a father," he said. "It's not even in the realm of something I ever considered." He took a sip of his drink, his throat suddenly parched.

Everywhere he looked he saw children. Babies. Lots of babies.

What Lily was going to have very soon.

One was bawling, red-faced and squirmy in her dad's arms. The crying reminder that Lily was a package deal had him feeling like the trees were closing in on him. He needed air, even though he was outside. He had to slip away, quietly, and just suck in some breaths.

"That's what you get for bringing a nine-months-pregnant woman to a party for one-year-olds," Lily said before he could move. "Mistaken for a husband and father and family man." She glanced away, then turned to him. "At Lamaze the other day, I liked that people there might have thought we were together. A family. I never get to feel that way."

He almost choked on his seltzer.

Lily gave him a pat on the back. And looked furious.

"Oh, fills you with dread, huh?" she said.

Uh-oh. "Lily, we've talked about this. Very recently. I never planned on becoming a father. I don't see myself in that role."

"Role? It's not like being a businessman. It's about how you feel. Committing because you want to."

But I don't want to, he thought. He looked at Ford with his baby son. At Axel with his baby daughter. At the toddlers racing around. Small children who had fathers here. These were families.

This isn't who I am.

"I have a craving for macaroni salad," Lily said and stomped off toward the buffet table.

Oh no. How had they gone from being guests at a party with pin the tail on the donkey hanging on a tree to having an argument? He didn't like tension between him and Lily. Then again, tension was always brewing beneath the surface. He just didn't like to think about it.

"Didn't mean to eavesdrop," Ford said as he stepped over. "But I actually heard all that."

Gavin let out a sigh and dropped his head back.

"I'm just gonna say," Ford began, shifting the baby he held, "that if I changed my mind about getting married and having a baby, if my wife did—then trust me, anyone can. Even you."

"I don't know, Ford," Gavin said, staring at the ground for a moment. "A family was never part of my plan. At any point in the future. I live on the road. I like it that way."

"Do you?" he asked.

Gavin stared at him for a second. Did he? Not having a home base had grown old a long time ago, but Gavin still had never bought anything. He'd kicked around the idea of having his own ranch, not a working one, since he wouldn't be around, but the idea of owning a ranch always reminded him of Harlan Mandeville. And the thought of a boxy condo didn't interest him. So he'd never bought anything. Just more luggage.

He strained his neck to see where Lily was, but he didn't spot her by the buffet table. He had to talk to her. He had to make things right between them. Not that he'd said anything he hadn't before.

But they kept kissing—and last night, even though she'd pulled away before their mouths could meet, they'd embraced. With feeling. Serious feeling. And if he didn't intend to be part of her and her baby's lives when Micah was born, he had to stop it. He felt furious at himself for giving in to the moment when the big picture was so important. What a jerk he'd been. Thoughtless.

And apologizing would just make things worse. She knew how he felt. She knew him. What Lily wanted, needed, was for him to change.

And he couldn't.

He moved away from the crowd toward a shady tree and took a breather. He heard footsteps and was relieved when it was Ford.

"It's a lot, I know," Ford said, nodding toward the party. "Especially if you're not used to babies and toddlers who could best you in the mile."

"And you all look really damned happy," Gavin said.

"We are. We have these huge family dinners with little people crawling all over us, our plates are always cold by the time we get to take a bite, someone's always crying, someone wants their mama and not their daddy. A lot. But worth every second."

He suddenly saw himself sitting in his makeshift office at whatever ranch he was consulting for, barely knowing anyone. The owner a little, maybe the foreman. But he was always on his own. And once he'd lost his mother, he made it a point to travel during the holidays. Last Christmas he'd been alone in Germany. His last birthday he almost forgot about until his most used credit card sent him an e-greeting.

But that was his life and how he was comfortable. He liked the distance—emotional and otherwise. He liked the quiet. He liked the combination of numbers and cattle and horses taking center stage in his head because there was nothing else. He could focus solely on his work, which enabled him to be fast. And good. He particularly liked not feeling like hell because the woman he'd fallen for was also sleeping with the owner of the ranch he was working for. He'd long pushed the thought of having a family out of his head. Giving up on romance was newer, but still felt right. He just wanted to be on his own.

His life on the road was the life he'd chosen. This? Being at this party. Being at the Wild Canyon? This was temporary.

This was a promise to Lily.

"Have you made a decision about the Wild Canyon?" Ford asked. "You going to keep it or sell it?"

Gavin slugged down the rest of his drink. "You know what? Keep this between us," he said. "But I just decided. I'm going to sell it."

He heard a gasp and turned to the right.

Lily stood there, her expression a combination of hurt and anguish and anger, with orange slices on a little plate, which slipped out of her hand and onto the grass.

"Lily," Gavin said, taking a step toward her. He had to explain.

But she grabbed at her belly and cried out, Sadie and Danica rushing over.

"I think I'm in labor," she managed to say, crying out again.

Micah Benjamin Augustus Gold—named for Lily's dad and both grandpas—seven pounds, six ounces, was born just before 8:00 p.m. Between labor and her OB placing her newborn son on her chest, Lily had forgotten anything else in her life existed except for the baby and her overwhelming love for him.

He was healthy and utterly beautiful. Lily's mother had been in the delivery room with her, puffing out her cheeks the way she'd learned in the three Lamaze classes she'd gone to. Gavin had called her shortly after Lily had said she thought she was in labor, the plate tumbling out of her hand. Lily would have dropped to the ground too if Gavin hadn't rushed to her and held her up as he led her to his SUV. Ford and Rex Dawson had given them a police escort, since an ambulance might have taken longer. She'd huffed and puffed the distance to the hospital, and by the time she'd been greeted at the entrance by a wheelchair and a kind-faced nurse, all she could think about was her baby.

After Micah was taken away to be cleaned up and weighed and wrapped in a blanket, Lily heard Gavin's words again—*I just decided. I'm going to sell it*—but her exhaustion had that beat. She couldn't even toss them over in her head. If he sold the ranch, so be it. She'd be fine. She always landed on her feet. She always had.

And now she was someone's mother, so hell yes, she'd be okay.

Her mom had stepped out to slug down a quick cup of coffee and tell Lily's gram that she was now a great-grandmother. When she returned, Tamara let her know that Gavin was pacing the waiting room, which was very crowded with Dawsons and Wild Canyon staffers, including Jonah and Aria and even eighty-seven-year-old Bill Pearson, who'd been in the cafeteria with his guardian angel ranch hand when the news had spread and had asked if he could come too. Her mom said that when she'd entered the waiting room, everyone had stood, excited to hear how much Micah weighed and how long he was and if he had any hair or not, and then there'd been a mad rush to the gift shop.

The next thing Lily knew, she was in a different room, a private room. She rang the bell attached to her bed and asked the nurse to bring her son. Lily sobbed the moment Micah was placed in her arms in his tiny striped cap. Her mother and grandmother poked their heads in the door, and they spent the next twenty minutes oohing and aahing over every inch of him.

He looked just like Lily, everyone said, and even Lily could see that was true. He had blond wisps and huge blue eyes and she could see her face in his.

"Gavin's been out there since he brought you here," her mother said. "He asked if he could see you—visiting hours will end pretty soon."

Lily looked down at her son. "I don't know if I want to see him." She wanted to tell her mom what she'd overheard Gavin say about selling the Wild Canyon, but all that would do was worry her mom, who'd tell her grandmother. The ranch meant the world to them.

She might be a brand-new mother, exhausted like she'd never been, pains in strange places, but hell yeah, she was about to give Gavin Dawson a huge piece of her mind.

"Actually, Mom, could you tell him to come in? I do want to talk to him, after all."

Tamara Gold raised an eyebrow at Lily's no

doubt fierce expression and hurried out. Lily carefully cradled Micah against her chest, marveling at the very sight of him. Her baby.

In moments, there was a knock and then Gavin came in, looking gorgeous and tired, holding a gift bag from the hospital shop with one long, fuzzy tan ear poking out of it.

"Wow," he said, staring from the baby to her and back to Micah. He set the gift bag on the table. His green eyes were soft on Micah, then on her. "He's a wonder, Lily."

"Yes, he is. And he reminds me what really matters. Him. Nothing else. You want to sell the Wild Canyon? It doesn't mean anything to you? Well, I guess I had it wrong about you, Gavin Dawson. So go ahead, bub. Sell it. I'll be fine. We'll all be fine." But she was a hormonal mess and tears dripped down her face. She dashed them away with the back of her free hand.

"Lily," he said, pulling a chair close to the edge of the bed. "I didn't mean to blurt that out about selling. I'd decided in that moment. Right there and then. I'm selling the Wild Canyon to you. For a dollar."

She gaped at him. "What?"

"You're the connection between me and Harlan Mandeville, Lily. You. I want you to have the ranch. You can hire someone to manage it and—"

Wait. Just. A. Minute. "Oh, so you're going to sign the ranch over to me and leave, huh? Just like that? Nope. Sorry. Not happening."

"What do you mean?" he asked, looking from her to Micah and then back at her. "Your future will be secure. As will your mother's and grandmother's. And Micah's. That's what I want, Lily. For you to have everything you need and want."

She wanted to grab a pillow and throw it at him. She needed and wanted him. "You made me a promise. That you'd wait six more weeks. Till I was back from my maternity leave before you made any decisions. So you can't sell the ranch to me until then."

He tilted his head.

"I've got my hands full, Gavin. You're going to add the Wild Canyon on top of this?" she asked, looking down at her baby's precious face, his tiny closed eyes. "You owe me six more weeks."

He nodded. "Six weeks. Okay. I won't do a thing until you're back at your desk. And if you need a couple weeks more, you just say so."

She really wanted that pillow. To bop him over the head with.

"He's everything, Lily," he said, his gaze on Micah. "Congratulations."

"He is everything," she whispered. She looked

up at Gavin. "Why are you selling the ranch to me for a dollar? It means that little to you?"

"It means that much," he said.

She bit her lip, trying to understand, but she was too damned tired. Her mind was blank except for Micah.

"Your mom brought your hospital bag," he said. "But if you need anything, you just say the word and I'll get it from your apartment or I'll buy it for you."

"I appreciate that," she said, yawning. She was so, so tired. Overwhelmed. By having her baby. By Gavin.

The nurse came in and said it was time to take Micah to the nursery for his pediatrician's visit. It was so hard to let him go.

A refrain she knew all too well.

She gave Micah a kiss on the forehead and watched the nurse leave with her heart.

Gavin took her hand. "I'm sorry I upset you to the point you went into labor," he said, his jaw tight, his eyes heavy. He shook his head.

"My doctor had said I could go into labor any minute. You surprised me, Gavin, but it's not like I wasn't prepared for you to come to that conclusion about the ranch. That you were going to walk away. I just hoped for different. But that's me. Lily-Hope-for-Different-Gold."

He brushed a tendril of her hair back from her face, his hand so comforting.

You can't leave us, she thought as she felt herself drifting off. *I already love you.*

Chapter Twelve

Gavin paced the living room of his house, Buddy watching him from his plush bed by the sliding glass doors in the living room. The moment he'd said the words out loud to Lily, that he was going to sell the ranch to her for a buck, he knew it was the right thing to do, what he wanted to do. It would solve all his problems. Lily would have her home and the ranch for security for the rest of her life, something special to pass on to Micah. And Gavin would be rid of the place.

"But what am I gonna do with you?" he asked Buddy. "Take you with me to strange ranches where you'll have to make friends with the other

ranch dogs and then leave in a few weeks for another ranch?" He went over to the dog's bed and
sat down, then hugged his knees to his chest. He
gave Buddy a good scratch on his side. "Maybe
Lily will want to keep you here. But she has a baby
now, Buddy. A baby and a dog? You're definitely
no trouble. But it's a lot to ask." He'd put the subject off. Just like he was putting off a lot.

He grabbed his phone and reread the text Lily's
mother had sent him. When he'd gotten home from
the hospital, he'd texted her to ask if there was anything, anything at all, big or small, that Lily still
needed for Micah or the nursery or just in general.
Tamara had texted back a list of about eleven items
and signed off with this message.

I figure if you asked, you meant it, so I've linked
her wish list at BabyCentral. Most of it had been
purchased so what's left are more want than need.
You're a wonderful person, Gavin Dawson.

That was up for debate. Lily certainly didn't
think so. Anymore. Which made him feel like hell.

He called up her wish list at BabyCentral and
ordered everything on it, then looked under the
Gifts for Newborns heading. He scrolled through
until he came across the personalized section and
ordered a baby blanket with Micah's name and

birth date across it, paying a small fortune for rush delivery on Monday, which was when a nurse said she and Micah would likely be discharged. He'd picked up a stuffed bunny from the hospital gift shop so as not to show up in her room empty-handed, but he'd wanted to get something a little more special, a little more personal.

A baby blanket with a name and birth date was hardly personal, though. Anyone could order that. Lily would probably receive ten of them.

More personal would be a real relationship with the family of two. To be by their side. Forever.

Again, his chest felt tight and he walked over to the sliding glass doors and stepped out, the April night air cool on his skin, which suddenly was too hot.

He pictured the nursery in Lily's apartment, where they'd had their first kiss of all places, and tried to imagine himself putting a baby down to sleep. Singing a lullaby. Sitting in the rocking chair and reading a bedtime story. Changing a diaper. Getting little arms and legs into clothing.

He could see himself doing all of that. But to help Lily. She'd need help, even with her mother and grandmother and good friend Brianna rallying around her.

What he couldn't see himself doing was walking away from her and Micah. Walking away the way his own father had. Micah wasn't his child, but he cared about that baby. He cared about Lily. No way was he just going to turn his back on them.

So you're going to propose to Lily and become Micah's dad? he asked himself. *Because that's what you're saying. And you have no intention of doing either.*

He felt a nudge against his leg and looked down to find Buddy sitting beside him. He knelt down and petted the dog's head and side, then buried his face in his soft hair. "I don't know what the hell I'm doing here, Buddy. Everything I want is at odds. So what do I do?"

Buddy remained silent.

"I'm not even supposed to be here, Buddy. I inherited this place from a man who had no interest in knowing me. Who left my mother in the lurch. Who made me question everything that should have been a birthright. I need to be back on the road." He'd reschedule his trip to Cheyenne and turning around the Six Winds Ranch until the promised six-week period was up. He wouldn't go back on that promise. Especially because he'd made it a second time tonight. But he had a commitment to that ranch, and his life was mobile and he'd be leaving. Having that settled calmed him down some.

And made his chest squeeze even tighter.

Nothing was right about any of this. Nothing felt right.

All he knew was that Lily mattered to him. A lot. And now Micah did too.

Two days later, Lily was ready to bring Micah home, but both her mother and her grandmother had colds—very bad timing, there, universe.

"I'm so sorry, sweetheart," her mother said over the phone. "I can't believe this. Neither Gram or I have been sick all year, and on my big day as Nana to bring my grandson home, whammo. I'm stuck in bed with tissues listening to your gram cough."

"Just focus on getting better," she said. "I'll be just fine."

"Of course you will. Because I sent Gavin to pick you up two up. He should be there any minute. He said he was happy to do it."

Happy? A nice word for her mom, but she was sure Gavin was not comfortable picking up a mother and child from the hospital and bringing them home.

"I'll call you later to check in," Lily said. "Just take care of yourself and Gram too, okay?"

"Of course. The sooner we're better, the sooner we can fuss over our Micah."

There was a rap at the door and Gavin poked his head in.

"We're all set," she said, slowly swinging her legs over the side of the bed as she cradled her son carefully in her arms. She had the discharge papers for both herself and Micah and they were good to go. "I can't thank you enough for picking us up. I'm sorry my mom bothered you, though. I could have called Brianna or Aria. You're probably very busy."

"No trouble in the slightest," he said, his smile warm and sincere. He looked at Micah. "Fast asleep, huh?"

"He likes his rest," she said on a yawn. "I got a good catnap in a few hours ago, so I feel pretty good right now. I'm just excited to get home and show him the nursery." She stood up and headed for the infant car seat her mom had brought over yesterday. Her gram had bought it for her as a shower gift a few months ago. "Would you mind putting him in the seat?" she asked. "I'm not at bending stage just yet."

His expression almost made her laugh. One part shock, one part horror.

"Or if you just lift the carrier on the bed, I can do it," she added.

"I've got it," he said, stepping closer, his expression more fear based.

"You won't drop him," she said. "I trust you."

She did, she realized.

He sucked in a breath. "I've never held a baby before."

"Here," she said. "Hold out your arms close to your body and I'll transfer him, and just use both hands and keep him cradled against you. You'll know when he feels secure."

He took Micah into his arms, and she realized she'd meant what she said. She did trust him. Every time a nurse had taken him from her the past two days, she'd felt that moment of apprehension, that someone else was taking her baby. But with Gavin, she felt none of that.

"He's so light," Gavin whispered, glancing at her and then back down at the baby.

"He's wearing pj's that Jonah and Aria bought him. If my mom were here, I would have put him in one of the thousands she'd bought, but how cute are those little cowboy and cowgirl silhouettes?"

"Pretty darn cute," he said. "I like the cowboy hats along the zipper too."

"Jonah even held him," she said. "He was sitting down the whole time, and he could only handle about thirty seconds, but he held him. It was so sweet. I think Aria teared up."

"I think those two are gonna be just fine," he said. "Eventually. But just fine."

"Yeah. Not sure about us," she said—without

meaning to. "Oh God. Did that just come out of my mouth?"

He looked at her, his expression now…somewhere between stricken and just heavy.

"I'll unbuckle the harness of the seat," she said, rushing over and getting that done.

He very gently laid the baby down. Micah quirked up one side of his mouth.

"That's my favorite thing that he does," she said, her eyes stinging with tears—half at the utter perfection of her baby boy and half at this frustrating man beside her.

You can't make someone love you.

Except sometimes she truly believed that Gavin did love her. Not wishful thinking, not fantasizing. The way he looked at her. The way he treated her. The way he planned to sell the Wild Canyon to her for a dollar.

But if he loved her, he wouldn't be leaving. He'd keep the ranch. He'd get down on one knee and propose because he was madly in love with her and they'd own the ranch together. They'd be a family.

She mentally shook her head. She was not going to do this. She was going to focus on her newborn. She was going to be a single mother, and she was everything to Micah.

Lily adjusted Micah's cap. "I think he'll be okay

in just the fleece pj's to get to the car if you bring it around front."

He nodded and took the bag. "All set, then?"

Except for you, she thought. *Except for your heart, blocked by a brick wall.*

When Gavin pulled up in front of the entrance to Lily's apartment, there were balloons and blue streamers everywhere and a banner on the lawn: Welcome Home, Micah!

"Aw," she said from the back where she was beside Micah's car seat. "How much crying can one new mother do?"

"A lot of people really care about you," he said.

His words—and then Lily's—came back to him. *I think those two are gonna be just fine*, he'd said. *Eventually. But just fine.*

Yeah. Not sure about us.

He could tell she hadn't meant to blurt that out. Or maybe she had, but then she'd rushed to change the subject, get Micah all buckled in and she'd given him an out.

He wished he could set her mind at ease, but he couldn't. How could he, when everything inside him was so jumbled? He knew he cared deeply for Lily. And now Micah. But leaving when his time was up—he felt that like a lifeline.

That was telling. And made him feel like hell.

"I can't wait to show Micah his home," Lily said. She opened the back door, and Gavin hurried out and around to her side to help her exit. "I thought I'd feel less pregnant. I mean, I do. But jeez, this is not the insta back to regular I thought it would be, even two days later. Oh Lord, why I am telling you all this?"

He smiled and gave her hand a squeeze. "Well, I'm here for you. Whatever you need."

She gave him something of a smile and then leaned in to unlatch the rear-facing carrier and pull it out. "Hi, my sweet baby boy!"

He could still feel the tiny weight of the newborn in his arms. He hadn't expected Micah to seem so sturdy.

Lily held the carrier with two hands. He got out her bag and followed her to the porch steps, where a package lay by the door. "Ooh, from BabyCentral. Someone sent me something!"

"I think it might have been me," he said. "I ordered something to be delivered today. Just a little something for Micah."

"Very thoughtful of you," she said. "I can't wait to see what it is."

He stopped for a second, extremely aware that her voice was too bright, that she was keeping things light and off them. She shouldn't have to work this hard, he thought. Not for him. Not to protect herself. The woman just had a baby. This was all so unfair to her.

Again, he felt like hell.

"I'll grab it for you." He scooped it up and opened the door.

"My mother and grandmother stocked the fridge and freezer and pantry and cleaned the place from head to toe yesterday," she said. "I won't have to cook for a year or clean for at least a month."

"I hope they both feel better soon. Your mom sounded so upset to miss the big day of you bringing Micah home."

"Aw, well, there will be lots of moments, big and small."

This was big. Very big. And he was glad he was here. He wanted to tell her that. But he was constantly contradicting himself, not making sense. He had to be careful with this woman he cared about so much.

"Micah," she said, holding up the carrier. "This is the living room. Those sliding glass doors lead to the deck and our backyard. If you hear barking, that's Buddy, Gavin's dog. He only barks when he sees a squirrel or chipmunk, so no worries about getting woken up from your naps."

"I told Buddy he has the important job of guarding over Micah," Gavin said.

Lily smiled. "C'mon, Micah. I'll show you the

nursery. It's right down this hall." She glanced at his face. "Still fast asleep, huh? You're missing the whole grand tour."

Gavin laughed. "You can do it all over again when he wakes up."

In the nursery, Lily explained to the baby what everything was, from the bassinet to the crib to the rocking chair to the bookcase to the rug. She set the carrier on the changing table and carefully took Micah out, her face full of wonder.

"It's not just me, right?" she asked, her blue eyes shining, her face having never looked more beautiful. "He really is a magical creature. Just absolute perfection," she added on a whisper. "Look at that adorable little nose. That sweet chin."

Gavin smiled, the emotion in her voice getting him a little choked up too.

"Let's see if I can put him in the bassinet without waking him up," she said. "That's my goal of the day. If I do that, I can eat ice cream for dinner, which I plan to, anyway."

"I'll scoop regardless," he said on a nod.

She smiled again and very slowly set the baby down in the bassinet. It was polished wood and looked like a one of a kind piece. "Harlan had this made for me. He gave it to me just a week before he died. He said it was made in the mountains by a gifted wood carver and would bring the baby luck and good health."

"It's a beautiful bassinet," Gavin said.

"Look! I did it!" she whispered, stepping back. "He's still asleep!"

He grinned. "Ice cream it is." He wanted to pull her into his arms and hold her, tell her he was sorry, tell her how much she meant to him. But he stayed where he was, giving her the distance she actually needed.

She looked at the package in his hand. "Can I open that now?"

"Sure," he said, handing it to her.

She sat down with an "ahhh" in the padded rocker and ripped open the mailer. "I wonder what it could be. It's not hard or very thick or bulky. Hmm." She reached in and pulled out the gift, wrapped in coated tissue paper. "Oh, Gavin," she said as she opened it, letting the blanket unfold down onto her lap. "It's an embroidered baby blanket with his name and birth date. It's so soft. And I love the shade of blue. I love the blanket so much. Thank you."

"You're very welcome."

"I'll always keep it right here on the rocker." She held it up again and smiled, then neatly folded it over the arm of the chair.

And before he could say another word, she too was fast asleep, her mouth slightly open.

He watched her sleep for a few minutes. There was another chair in the corner by the window, overstuffed and with an ottoman, and Gavin sank onto it. Like Buddy, he'd keep guard.

A sharp cry woke him up, Lily already bolting up and rushing to the bassinet. Micah let out another cry and Lily had him in her arms, one hand carefully supporting his neck and head. He glanced at the time on his phone. A little over an hour had passed.

"I've got you, precious," she said to the baby. "Everything is okay. Hungry? Diaper wet?"

Gavin sat up straighter, then stood up.

She froze, as if she didn't realize he was still even in the room. "I was sure you'd left."

"Nope," he said. "I'm happy to stay, get you what you need. I know I'm not exactly your mom or gram, but I've got two hands."

She glanced down at Micah, then looked at him. "I can't, Gavin. I can't pretend you're something you're not. Like part of my life. In a few weeks you're planning to leave. So I can't have you here, acting like you care deeply about the two of us. Like you're part of this little family. If you're here, helping and enmeshed in our lives, especially these early days, it'll hurt too much when you go. So just go now."

Knife to the heart. Punch to the gut.

"Lily, I—"

She gave a slight shake of her head. "Unless you're suddenly 'and Gavin makes three,' you should go. I'm a single mother. This is my life. This is my life's work. I've got this."

He sucked in a breath, his head, his heart, all of him a jumble. He didn't want to leave. He couldn't make his legs move. "If you need anything, you text me. Or call me. Anything at all. Day or night. Three a.m. I'm right next door."

She nodded.

Walking out of that nursery was harder than he ever thought it would be.

Chapter Thirteen

The first week of motherhood: Lily was either scared she was doing something wrong, napping because Micah was, or researching what every cry and coo he made was about. Lily's mother and grandmother were on the mend and both cleared by their doctors to spend time around the baby by the third day she was home. Gavin checked in every few hours. He stopped by every single night with a small gift for Micah—whether a pacifier or a cute rattle or a little baby book. She was too physically tired and mentally and emotionally ex-hilarated by her newborn to focus on her broken heart, but her chest hurt. According to Gavin, Aria was doing such a great job in the office that he wasn't going to replace Lily until she was ready to return. Lily didn't want to think about what that meant. That she'd be the owner of the Wild Canyon and would likely want to hire her own admin.

The second week: much of the same.

The third week: Lily was still exhausted but felt better overall. Gavin still checked in every day, as was his way, and dammit if she didn't appreciate it. He still brought Micah little gifts and Lily her favorite sandwich from the diner or bath salts or a foot massager. Sometimes when he left, Lily would burst into tears, her feelings for him and their situation overwhelming. And sometimes she felt strong and "you don't know what you're missing, bub." Sometimes she felt both in the same second.

The fourth week of motherhood: Lily had come to understand that her schedules were just about useless. Sometimes Micah slept for forty minutes, sometimes for three hours. She was up all night, her mom doing the midnight shift but needing to get her rest so that she could be of help during the day. Lily's own naps were all over the place, and she often woke up feeling groggy. And various parts of her body were aching less. Her OB had mentioned that she could have sex at the six-week mark, and Gavin's gorgeous face and long, lean, muscular body snapped into her mind, but she couldn't imagine having sex. Yet.

And if she slept with Gavin Dawson, she'd be a goner. She could barely handle the hot kisses they'd shared.

Which had come to a stop, of course. Everything between them had. She heard from Aria and friends around the Wild Canyon that he was "exceptionally present" on the ranch these past four weeks, visiting the programs and initiatives that she'd dragged him here to finalize, working closely with the foreman, riding along every acre of the property to inspect and make notations. He'd even stopped in a few times to check on Bill Pearson and had bought him a new series of Westerns. She knew this because Daniel McJones, the ranch hand who owed Bill his life, had happened to be there when Gavin had dropped in with the books. Apparently, Bill had thanked Gavin profusely for thinking of him but said, "They don't write Westerns the way they used to like when I was a teenager." Daniel had chuckled and said he could see those shiny new books staying unread on Bill's bedside table while he made his trips to the library to take out the old series from, like, a half century ago that he'd read over and over.

And per her grandmother, who had hired an extra cook since Lily's mom was only working at the caf a couple hours here and there while she focused on her grandbaby, Gavin ate in the cafeteria at least once a day and always asked about her great-grandson and if there were any milestones.

There were constant milestones. Ones that Lily decided were unique to Micah alone, like interesting facial expressions that she couldn't quite call a smile.

She loved her baby son more than anything in the world. Motherhood filled her up, but now that she was more used to the huge change in her life and her days, she was more and more aware of how much she missed Gavin. How much she wished he were here, asleep on that overstuffed chair in the nursery. Sometimes, she'd see Buddy snoozing on the porch as she passed the main house with Micah in his stroller, and she'd get such a pang.

Her husband. Their baby. Their dog.

But that wasn't going to happen, and she'd been trying hard to accept it.

Like right now, as she was taking Micah for a walk in his infant stroller and saw Gavin coming up the path in his dark brown Stetson, so sexy in those jeans and boots.

"How's the little guy?" he asked, peering over the stroller and smiling at Micah.

He was awake, his blue eyes focused on Gavin.

"He's doing great," Lily said. "We had a great one-month checkup this morning."

"Glad to hear it. He looks so much like you, Lily."

She loved hearing that. Micah truly did look like her, no reminders of his biological father. But when she was supposed to be catching her naps, she'd think about those questions that had come up when she'd first met Gavin. When Micah would be, say, three years old, and ask where his daddy was. Those thoughts would keep her from sleeping.

"Remember when Harlan's lawyer told me he'd bring over an accordion file that Harlan had left for me but couldn't give me until the five-week mark of his passing?" Gavin asked.

Lily tilted her head. "I do remember."

"Well, the attorney reminded me this morning that it's been well past the five-week mark and that he was personally delivering it this afternoon at four since I might not otherwise ever pick it up. Jonah reminded me too. I stopped by the sanctuary to check in and see how the senior horses settled in and the two new goats. Jonah mentioned he couldn't believe it had been almost two months since Harlan had died and how everything and nothing had changed."

"I see Jonah hasn't changed," she said with a

smile. "He has found a lot of reasons to stop by the office, though. I can see the path from my apartment, so I know he comes by to see Aria."

"I have no doubt they'll find their way to each other," he said, holding her gaze.

Lily didn't let out the wistful sigh building in her chest. If only she and Gavin could find their way to each other. But if the miracle of Micah hadn't knocked any sense into Gavin or dislodged any of those bricks surrounding his heart, then she supposed nothing would.

There were two weeks left of the agreement. Six weeks from the day Micah was born.

She had to let Gavin Dawson go. That was just the way it had to be.

But Micah had other ideas. As Gavin trailed a finger along his hand, the baby wrapped his fist around Gavin's pointer finger.

Gavin stared at the little fist, surprise lighting his face. "Wow. That is some grip."

Oh, Gavin, she thought—for the millionth time, perhaps. Even a four-week-old knows you belong here. With us.

But would Gavin ever believe that?

Gavin sat at his desk in his office, his mind on Lily to the point that when Aria buzzed him to let him know that the attorney had arrived, he'd completely forgotten.

Something else was on his mind. The way Micah had grabbed onto his finger with his tiny fist. How could a newborn be so strong? That was a mighty grip. If Lily hadn't distracted the baby with a quick round of peekaboo, Micah might not have let go.

He still felt the imprint of that fist around his finger. *You're mine*, that grip had said. *Mine.*

Gavin leaned his head back, unable to process what he was thinking, feeling.

Lily. Micah. Lily. Micah. The two of them, the beautiful family, filled his head at all hours no matter what he was doing. Woke him up from sleep. Interfered with his work. The worst was when he visited the cafeteria and Lily's mother and grandmother would come over, making a fuss over him, showing him photos on their phones of Micah and many of Lily and Micah.

We've got that online profile all written up, her mom had said yesterday. *We'll wait till Micah's six weeks since everyone knows that's when she might be ready to start dating, but we won't spring that on her yet.* She added a sly smile and air quotes around the word *dating*, which Gavin took to mean she was talking about Lily's sex life making a return. The thought of her with another guy had cost him his appetite.

Someone else kissing her? Touching her? Someone pushing Micah's baby stroller. He couldn't see it. Didn't want to.

But in the same thought, he pictured himself on the road, at the Six Winds Ranch in Cheyenne, where he was due in two weeks. Back to his life. One far away and far removed from the Wild Canyon and Lily Gold. And Micah.

He went to the door and opened it and welcomed in Lamont Jones, who was carrying the accordion folder.

"This is all there is," the man said. "I don't have anything to accompany it, words that Harlan asked me to say, a letter to give you. Just the folder. But here it is," he added, handing it over.

Gavin took the folder, which wasn't very bulky. He couldn't tell by feel what it might contain. And honestly, he wasn't even sure he wanted to know. Something felt complete with the transfer of the folder, a final piece of his stay at the Wild Canyon. Now that he had the folder, and with two weeks left of his agreement with Lily, he would soon be free to go, free to take his life back and direct it how he wanted instead of Harlan Mandeville having the reins. Which was how it had felt these past weeks. Now it was over.

When the lawyer left and Gavin closed the door, he gave the folder another feel, thinking he'd be able to tell what was inside, but the thing felt almost weightless, as though it contained some documents and nothing more.

He sat down and turned his chair around, looking out at the majestic stables. Then he opened up the bottom desk drawer and put the accordion folder inside and shut it. All he knew was that he wasn't ready to open it. And he didn't know when he'd be. Maybe never.

There was another rap on the door. Aria was only here until four thirty today. Maybe it was Lily. He stood up and went to the door, hoping to see her beautiful face.

But it was Jonah.

"Got a minute?" Jonah asked, pushing his mop of brown hair off his forehead.

"Sure. Come on in."

Jonah leaned against the credenza, so Gavin leaned against his desk, trying to set the guy at ease.

"I keep thinking how Harlan died more than a month ago," Jonah said.

Gavin nodded. "How are you doing?"

"I'd be doing better if I knew you weren't going to sell the Wild Canyon."

"I can't really talk about that right now, Jonah. But I can promise you that—"

"You can't promise anything if you can't even talk about it," Jonah snapped. "What's the point? Why do I even bother? Now I'm all completely attached to those ridiculous llamas and you're just gonna sell the place to some soulless corporation. Forget it all. Nothing lasts."

"I don't believe that's true. Some things go, yes. But some things—" Are keepers, he wanted to say. Yet he didn't believe that. Nothing was a keeper. For a while there, he'd had his mother as his family, and of course she was a keeper. A great mom. But he'd lost her. And then he'd gotten his heart walloped and he'd stopped seeking connection.

And Jonah was similar, except that he couldn't help finding connection—with the senior animals at the sanctuary. With Aria. Who he was keeping at serious arm's length.

"Everything dies or just goes away," Jonah said. "Everything."

"Cycle of life," he said gently. "That doesn't mean you have to push away what you care about, who you care about."

"You care about Lily and you're leaving. You care about Micah too. It's impossible not to be nuts about that baby. But you're leaving. So forget the lectures."

With that, Jonah huffed out.

Gavin let out a heavy sigh and went outside, needing the breeze on his face.

Jonah's words echoed in his head, slamming against each other. He meant what he'd said to the guy. But applying it to himself was another story. Jonah was young. Just turned twenty. He could change his way of thinking. But Gavin was ten years older, ten years wearier. And change didn't come easy.

Still, he couldn't stop thinking about the day he'd leave the Wild Canyon. How exactly he'd do that. Say goodbye to Lily and Micah and get in his truck and drive down the road and out through the gates? He'd just head off to Cheyenne and his next consulting gig and that would be that? Yeah, right.

One thing he wasn't, was naive. Leaving felt as wrong as staying.

In the morning, Gavin checked in with Lily via text and got back the usual emoji of the smiley face wearing the cowboy hat. Then he texted the foreman to ask how things had gone with one of the newborn calves last night and got good news that it had gone well.

Gavin had a meeting in town with a new attorney—not that he didn't like Harlan's guy just fine, but he preferred to choose his own—to go over the details of signing over the ranch to Lily. She hadn't brought it up since the day he'd blurted it out at the hospital. And he hadn't either.

It was the one thing he did know for sure. That he wanted her to have the ranch. That it should be hers.

By noon, he had the details he needed squared away and the paperwork prepared for her signature. He went into the coffee shop for some quick caffeine and ate half a lemon bar, then passed a gift shop, where he couldn't help stopping in to see if there was something Lily might like, something for Micah too. He left with a stretchy beaded bracelet for Lily that spelled out the baby's name; apparently, it could also be worn as an anklet. He'd decided against having it wrapped and said yes to a ribbon. Just a little something, not quite a gift.

He realized he was passing the library and thought of Bill Pearson, grumbling about the three Westerns he'd bought the man the last time he was in town. Bill had raised an eyebrow at the shiny new books, but Gavin understood. Bill was old-school. Since he was right here, he'd take out some books Bill would actually read.

He stopped at the reception desk and asked for the section of old-fashioned Westerns, probably paperbacks. He mentioned he knew an elderly fan and wanted to bring him a few to tide him over for the weekend.

"Oh, do you mean Bill Pearson?" the librarian asked. "There's a five-book series by his favorite author, and he's been rereading those the last month. He's got one and two right now, which he must have read fifty times over the years already, so if you want to bring him the next three, I'm sure he'd love that."

Gavin smiled. "Great. Thank you."

"Right over here to this rack," she said, giving the long carousel a swirl. "Ah. Here they are. Number three, four and five. The adventures of Harlan Something. I can never remember the name." She smiled and handed him the stack.

Gavin froze and stared at her. Harlan?

The librarian glanced down at the top book. "Ah, the series is called Range River Valley, but Bill told me Harlan is the lead cowboy. All the books are about him, apparently. Bill said he's like the Lone Ranger, that kind of thing."

Gavin took the books. He turned the top one over and read the description. "The Adventures of Harlan Mandeville, Cowboy Hero…"

The air whooshed out of Gavin's lungs. He could hear the librarian talking but was barely able to focus on her words.

"The books must be over seventy years old," she

was saying. "The author long moved on, but Bill sticks with this series. Every now and then he'll mix it up and read some older books by other authors, but he always comes back to Range River Valley."

And the adventures of Harlan Mandeville.

Gavin stood frozen, staring down at the books in his hand. The cover showed a young cowboy on a brown horse, a purposeful look in both their eyes.

Harlan Mandeville, Gavin's father, had been left on a doorstep with a note saying only that the baby's name was Harlan Mandeville. And according to Edgar in town, Harlan had once told him that was a made-up name. That was all Gavin knew, all anyone knew, unless Jonah knew more than he'd said, but Gavin didn't think so. It had been clear that Harlan didn't talk about his past and had only referenced being a "throwaway" because the animal sanctuary Lily had wanted to start at the ranch had reminded him of himself.

He looked down at the books in his hand.

Bill Pearson, in the old cabin, was the key to his father's past. The key to Gavin's. Answers to the questions he'd been thinking about his entire life.

But Gavin had dropped by three times since arriving in town, once with Lily and twice on his own to check in. Bill had never said a word about any connection to Harlan or that his favorite literary hero had the same name. Why wouldn't he mention something like that?

He couldn't get back to the ranch fast enough.

Chapter Fourteen

Gavin drove straight to the old cabin, but Bill wasn't there. There was a practically illegible note, from age and inclement weather, taped on the door that said *Out Walking*.

Dammit.

Gavin went looking for Daniel McJones, the ranch hand who looked after Bill, brought him groceries, took him to the library every couple of weeks. Finding one cowboy on a ranch the size of the Wild Canyon was impossible, so he texted the foreman, who gave him Daniel's location this morning. He was awaiting a hay delivery and was at the main barn.

Gavin headed there and found Daniel, who looked surprised the big boss wanted to see him. The man was about forty with short blond hair under a cowboy hat. He was tall and wiry, a blue-and-white bandanna around his neck.

Gavin extended his hand, and Daniel shook it. "Sorry to interrupt your work. I have a question about Bill Pearson."

"Bill? He okay?" Daniel asked.

"He's just fine. It's a really nice thing the way you make sure he's taken care of."

"I almost drowned in a flash flood," Daniel said. "Bill pulled me out. That was over twenty years ago. I don't know where he found the strength. He wasn't young then. I had at least twenty pounds on him and he worked part-time in the caf at the time, helping out. How the hell did he save my life? I'll never get over it. I do remember he said he learned everything he knew from the Westerns he reads." He shook his head. "I'm just grateful. As is my wife."

Gavin swallowed. Cowboy hero Harlan Mandeville had likely saved someone from a flash flood a time or two. And Bill had leaped into action, very likely recalling how Harlan had done it in the pages of his favorite series.

"You two ever talk about those Westerns he takes out of the library?" Gavin asked.

He shook his head. "Nah. I'm not much of a reader, though, so we don't talk books. I did ask him a couple times why he rereads the same old-timey books over and over, and he said he likes the main character, a real cowboy hero." He shrugged.

"I appreciate your time," Gavin said, and Daniel nodded and headed over to the delivery truck.

Gavin pulled out his phone and texted Lily, asking if she had time to talk, that he had some very interesting news.

I'm at the sanctuary with Micah, she texted back. Showing him the new horses.

Gavin left his truck by the main barn and walked down the path to the sanctuary, using the quarter mile to try to wrap his head around what he'd learned.

Could Bill Pearson be Harlan Mandeville's father? Harlan was seventy when he died. Bill was about to turn eighty-eight. If Bill was Harlan's father, he'd have been born when Bill was seventeen. It was entirely possible. But why would a teenage boy leave his newborn son on a doorstep with a made-up name, even the hero of his favorite series of Westerns?

Gavin found Lily in front of the horse pasture at the animal sanctuary, the stroller beside her, which was facing the horses, not that Micah could see much. Just around the side of the barn, he could see Jonah and Aria. They were facing each other, deep in conversation, their hands entwined.

Yes, he thought. Finally. Gavin wasn't sure if their recent conversation had had anything to do with Jonah breaking out of his comfort zone, but if his words had sunk into one of them, he was glad for Jonah.

"What's so interesting?" Lily asked as he walked up to her.

He told her about his trip to the library. To Bill's cabin. To meet with Daniel McJones.

And about his theory, that Bill might be Harlan's father.

Lily seemed to be taking in all she'd heard. "So he named his newborn son Harlan Mandeville after his favorite cowboy hero and left him on a doorstep?" Lily asked. "Who was the mother? Where was the mother? And if Bill is Harlan's father, Harlan definitely didn't know that all these years. I don't know that for sure, but I'd bet anything on the fact that he didn't know. Harlan gave Bill the cabin because he saved a ranch hand's life and that was Harlan's way, but he never gave Bill a passing look otherwise."

"All the theory does is raise more questions. I have to talk to Bill. I wonder why he never said anything to me, though. Not a word. He knows

I'm Harlan's son. And I've brought up Harlan. We talked about him the first time we stopped in."

"When was the first Harlan Mandeville Western written?" she asked. "The time frame matches?"

Gavin nodded. "I checked the copyright in the first pages. Published seventy-six years ago. Bill would have been eleven. I looked up the author and series too. Apparently the books were never very popular and went out of print and the author moved on to a different series, still Western. I suppose that's why no one's heard of Harlan Mandeville or made a connection between the cowboy hero and the note left with the baby on the doorstep. Or since."

Lily nodded. "Bill has a secret. A big secret. I'd give him a couple hours to get back home and then head over."

"Could you join me?" he asked slowly. *Because I need you there. I don't want to face this alone. I need you by my side.* He could feel the little gift box in his pocket, the beaded bracelet that spelled out Micah. Now didn't seem the right time to give it to her.

She peered at him. "Yes, of course. My mom will be thrilled to have Micah to herself for a while."

"Thanks," he said.

"Is Bill Pearson your grandfather?" she asked, wonder on her beautiful face.

Gavin stared at her, once again unable to process the thought. "We're going to find out, I guess."

"Oh, Gavin," she said, throwing her arms around him.

He stood there in the sunshine and wrapped his arms around her. "Wow, this feels very different without your belly between us."

She laughed. "Yeah, it does."

He could stand like this forever.

Lily had only been apart from Micah during naps and showers, and leaving her baby, even with her mom, for however long she'd be at Bill's wasn't as easy as she'd thought it would be. A little time to herself, an important mystery about to be solved—maybe. She was sure she'd be excited to have her mind and hands to herself.

But walking away from Micah was tough stuff. Getting in Gavin's SUV even harder.

"I already miss Micah," she said to Gavin as he headed toward the cabin.

"Fierce connection and intense bond," Gavin said. "I really appreciate that you're coming with me. I know it has to be hard leaving Micah, even for a half hour." He slowed the truck down so he could reach into his pocket. "Here's a little something that might help." He handed her a small box, like a jewelry box.

What was this? She undid the pretty ribbon. Inside the box was a stretchy beaded bracelet that spelled out Micah's name in black letters, followed by a little red heart. Her own heart squeezed in her chest. "I love this. Thank you."

"I thought you might like it," he said.

I thought you might like it. The more he thought of her, the kinder he was, the more she believed that he did love her. But maybe Gavin Dawson was just thoughtful, particularly to single mothers. Maybe she should stop reading so much into everything he did.

"I do," she said, looking at it on her wrist and loving the sweet connection to her son.

He smiled. "Think Bill will talk to me?"

"Good question. You should be prepared for him to clam up. He might not tell you anything. And if that's the case, he may come around in a day or two."

Gavin nodded. "I thought about that. But I'll start slowly, tell him the truth about the connection I made at the library between his literary hero and the name of my father and how there are no Mandevilles in the area, so it can't be a coincidence. And we'll see. If he doesn't respond, I'll just ask him straight-out. 'Are you Harlan's father?'"

Lily nodded. "I think that's a good plan. To give him a chance to talk without coming right out with the question."

When they arrived at the cabin tucked into the woods, the note was off the door.

"Ready?" Lily asked.

"I've had burning questions for years about Harlan. The why of this and that. When that door opens, I might finally have some missing pieces."

"The whys of Harlan's life," she said gently. Gavin's family.

He nodded. "Let's do this." He got out of the SUV with the three paperback books in his hand and came around to open her door. "Thank you, again, for doing this with me. For being here. There."

She gave his hand a squeeze. "As you say, anytime."

Gavin knocked on the cabin door. Bill opened it, standing there looking from Gavin to Lily.

"Been getting lots of visits lately," Bill said. He wore his usual outfit of baggy jeans, a button-down shirt and a leather vest over it. No hat right now. "Maybe too many."

Lily glanced at Gavin. She hoped that wasn't a sign of a bad mood, of too much company. Bill was a solitary person.

Lily looked closely at Bill, in a way she never

had before, for a family resemblance. He didn't look all that much like Harlan—or Gavin—except maybe in height. They were six feet or a few inches taller. Bill did have green eyes and so did Gavin. But Harlan's eyes had been hazel. There might be something in the expression that seemed similar— to Harlan and Gavin—but Lily might be looking for what wasn't there. She just wasn't sure.

Then again, Micah looked just like Lily, and she barely saw anything of his father in his face. That might be the case with Harlan and Gavin, that they favored their mothers.

"I stopped at the library today," Gavin said. "I asked the librarian for her recommendations for Westerns for you since you didn't seem to much like the new books, and she gave me three of your favorite series. About the adventures of Harlan Mandeville."

Bill stared at Gavin, his green eyes widening.

Lily almost gasped at the small but definite reaction yet tamped it down.

She could feel Gavin practically vibrating beside her.

But Bill didn't say anything. He just stood there and twisted his lips, then glanced away. "I have some things to do. Bye now," he said before closing the door.

Lily looked at Gavin. "Oh boy."

Gavin knocked again. "Bill, please. I've had un-answered questions my entire life. You can help."

"I don't know anything," Bill called through the door.

Lily could hear an internal door close, likely the bedroom where Bill had shut himself in.

"Well, at least we know it's not a coincidence," Gavin said. "But now what?"

"I think we have to wait till he comes to you," Lily said. "Give him some time. He's been keep-ing a secret for seventy years. I think he just needs to think it over and he'll come to you."

"I hope so," Gavin said.

She wondered if he was aware how much his entire world was going to blow open when Bill did come to him, and she had no doubt he would—eventually. But would the answers about Harlan's past change how Gavin looked at himself, viewed the world?

Or would he stay the lone wolf he claimed to be?

Except wolves moved in packs. And she and Micah, Aria and Jonah, and now Bill Pearson, were part of his pack.

She could let Gavin Dawson go, let him leave, or she could fight for him. And hadn't Lily said she got things done?

* * *

Twice, Gavin had gotten in his truck with plans to drive back to Bill's cabin, pound on the door and demand answers. And twice he'd gotten out of his truck and gone back inside. Lily was right. He had to give it time, had to let Bill come to him.

A knock at his door had him jumping to his feet. That was fast.

He expected to see Bill standing there, Daniel McJones's truck or one of the ranch utility vehicles driving off, but it was Lily on the porch.

Not looking particularly happy either. She was holding Micah, in orange-striped pj's and a matching cap, cradled against her.

"Is something wrong?" he asked.

"There's a delivery truck from BabyCentral in my drive," she said. "Except I didn't order anything. Apparently you had my entire wish list sent over."

He'd almost forgotten that he'd done that. "I just wanted you to have everything you needed."

"I do," she said. "I have the basics and then some. I got a slew of baby gifts the day Micah was born. Anything still on my wish list was a silly want."

"Well, those are good to have too," he said, not sure why she seemed angry. It was under the surface right now, but she seemed about to lose her temper.

"Is this for you to feel better about leaving?" she asked. "To provide for me and Micah so you don't have to give of yourself?"

He stared at her.

"I just want you to have everything, Lily. I care about you. And Micah. That's all I meant by ordering the rest of the wish list."

Micah started to fuss and Lily shifted him in her arms. Gavin reached out to touch his tiny hand, and again the baby grabbed onto Micah's finger, his pinkie this time, with his iron grip.

"Micah is staking a claim on you, Gavin Dawson," she said, looking from the baby's fist to Gavin. "And so am I. Regardless of what you find out about Harlan or Bill. I'm standing here telling you that I love you. That I want you to stay. That Micah and I want you to join our family. I don't want the ranch, Gavin. I want you."

The word *love* echoed in his head. Stay. Stay. Stay.

His skin felt tight. And clammy. "Lily, I…care about you. Very much. But—"

But what? He had no idea what he was saying. What he was doing. This woman was everything to him and he couldn't find words, couldn't even think. All he could latch on to was Micah's face. A baby. A child.

And his head just went blank. Not too long ago he'd been at a huge ranch, getting it out of impending trouble. He'd been living the life he wanted. Solo. No commitments. Just him and his truck.

Now he had a dog.

And a baby gripping his finger.

And the woman he cared about more than anything telling him she loved him. Asking him to stay.

And nothing was coming out of him. No words. He wasn't even sure there was any expression on his face.

"You mean so much to me, Lily. You and Micah both."

"But you're leaving. Giving me everything— my baby wish list, the Wild Canyon. Just not the one thing I really need. And really want. You."

Love. Family. He looked at the baby in her arms, then at her beautiful face and all he could feel was…something shuttering in his chest. He should be straight with her right now. She was asking and deserved the truth. Leaving had always felt like a lifeline. Right now, it did more than ever.

"I always planned to leave, Lily. You know that. You asked for six weeks after Micah's birth and I agreed, but I never thought those weeks would turn my mind around about this place. The Wild Canyon feels like hell, Lily. It has since I was old enough to know that this is where my father was, where he was walking around, not giving a flying rat that I existed. I hate this ranch, Lily."

He could see tears glistening in her eyes. "I don't believe that. I think you love this ranch. I think you've come to care about the employees too. I think you're just stuck in your head, unable to let go of the past."

He wasn't able to. And nothing in the accordion file and nothing Bill Pearson could say would change things. Yes, Harlan Mandeville had been left on a doorstep—whose, he still didn't know. Maybe an orphanage or a boys' home. He'd been named after a fictional character. He'd ignored the fact that he had a child.

Harlan hadn't been able to deal with his past. Just like Gavin couldn't deal with his. No commitments. No family. Just him.

Just like his father.

He hadn't even able to look in the accordion folder the lawyer had handed over.

Gavin leaned his head back and turned away. He hadn't ever seen himself like Harlan before, but suddenly he did and he didn't like it. He wasn't Harlan Mandeville. He'd never turn his back on his own child. And to make sure of that, just in case Harlan's blood ran strong in Gavin's veins, he long ago turned his back on the idea of marriage and fatherhood. To protect anyone he might hurt.

He shook his head at himself. It all sounded so…dumb now. When he thought it through, when he thought it out loud in his own head.

But he felt what he felt. Which was like a block-ade.

Lily looked the same spitting mad she had the day he'd met her, at the gates of the Dawson Family Guest Ranch. "Well, I've got news for you, bub," she said. "When you leave, you're leaving the best thing that ever happened to you. Me and Micah. And don't think I'm flattering myself. I just happen to know you better than you think I do. And I believe you love me, Gavin Dawson. I believe you love this little boy too. You're just being incredibly stubborn. Like Bill Pearson is right now."

"Lily—" But he didn't know what he wanted to say. He couldn't think. He needed air and he was standing outside.

"Micah doesn't seem interested in letting go of your pinkie," she said. "Guess you'll have to peel his fist off."

He looked down at the baby boy, whose eyes were open but slightly sleepy. "Or I could just stand here till he falls asleep."

She stared at him, her expression softening, but

he wasn't sure why. "That's how I know you love him," she said. "Because you won't let go yourself. You can't."

She carefully reached a hand to tickle Micah's fist and he let go of Gavin's pinkie.

Then she marched back around the side of the porch. The imprint of Micah's grip was still as strong as if the baby was holding on.

Chapter Fifteen

Lily couldn't take another second of her mother oohing and aahing over all the wish list items that had not so mysteriously arrived for her and were now all in place in the nursery at her mom's insistence. Yes, the furry chair that looked like a monkey was adorable. The wipe warmer meant Micah would never feel a cold wipe against his bare bottom—for heaven's sake, did she actually put that on her wish list? The pj's and onesies and shorts and tops and socks in the next size up that Lily'd had so much fun choosing and selecting for "one day" were what her wish list really was about. Not anything she or Micah actually needed. They'd already had the basics.

"So you're mad at him for being ridiculously generous?" her mother asked from the rocking chair, where she was making a pile of the new clothing to wash. "The man is your boss and rich as heck to boot. Who's going to buy out BabyCentral, if not him?"

That's when Lily started to cry. Big dumb fat tears rolling down her face.

Tamara set aside her pile and leaped up. "What's wrong?"

"Everything," Lily said, standing over Micah's bassinet and watching him sleep, which had helped enormously a couple of hours ago after she'd stormed off from Gavin. She'd tried—she'd fought for him, she'd told him how she'd felt. She'd even told him how he felt. But maybe she had it wrong. He just didn't love her. "I'm not supposed to do this. I'm supposed to focus on being the best mom I can be. On Micah. Not on how bad I feel over Gavin Dawson." She shook her head and then buried her face in her hands.

"Oh my goodness, you're in love with him," her mother said gently. "I could see the two of you were close, that you'd formed a bond. But I had no idea."

Lily dropped her hands and nodded. "He told me

he was leaving the Wild Canyon after I came back from maternity leave. So in a week, he's leaving."

"But what about the ranch?" Tamara asked.

"He's selling it to me. For a dollar. Apparently he's drawn up the paperwork because his lawyer called to ask if Lily Gold was my legal name."

Her mother's mouth dropped open. "He's selling the ranch to you for a dollar? What?"

Lily told her everything. Up to the part about Bill Pearson, which she thought was Bill's business at this point. Until the man talked to Gavin, Lily didn't want to bring him into it. She told her mother about the kisses. About how she'd stupidly fallen in love with a man who'd told her he was leaving the moment she was back on her feet.

"Well, I'm no expert about modern relationships, Lily, and my last kiss was your father and he's been gone awhile now, but I'll tell you this. Based on everything you just told me, everything I've seen with my own eyes, that man loves you right back. He's not going anywhere. Like you said, he's stuck in his head. Caring about people and places have a bad hold on him. I get that. But he's in love with you. And that'll be stronger than what's got him all twisted up inside."

"I don't know. I thought the exact same thing. But I really think he's going to leave. He can't get past what the Wild Canyon represents. And he can't let himself love anyone or anything. I thought maybe Micah would soften him up, make him see that he gets to decide how he feels and what he does about how he feels. But I think Micah just reminds him of himself, an innocent baby left behind."

"Micah is not left behind. He's got you. The way Gavin had his mother."

Lily nodded. "So maybe he just doesn't love us."

Suddenly Lily realized that would be the only thing that would keep Gavin from leaving. His true feelings. If he didn't love her.

And maybe he didn't.

He was too kind to say so when she'd told him she loved him. Too kind to peel her baby's fist off his finger. Too generous. Too everything.

Except willing to stay and be with her and Micah. To be a family.

I'm standing here telling you that I love you. That I want you to stay. That Micah and I want you to join our family. I don't want the ranch, Gavin. I want you.

Gavin sat in his office at the big desk, Lily's words going through his mind over and over. One moment, all she'd said would fill him up, make his heart feel like it was soaring, and then the next, icy dread would take over and he'd focus on leaving the ranch, leaving town.

Leaving Lily and Micah.

He had such admiration for her, the way she put herself out there, said what was on her mind. Spoke her truth. She was brave. And he was unable to take all she was offering. Love. A family. A future.

He stared at the drawer he'd shoved the accordion file in. What was in there? Something that would dislodge all this dread inside him? Or something that would make it all worse?

The age-old question that he'd never had an answer to. It was why he stayed on the road, he knew. Why he'd sworn off ever having a family of his own. Because there had never been an answer. So he'd never dug very far into Harlan Mandeville's life.

All this time, he'd had a grandfather right here in Bear Ridge, living his own version of Harlan's life. Gavin's life. Or they were living his.

Open the folder, he told himself. *Just do it.*

He grabbed it out of the drawer and set it on the desk and unwound the string. Inside were bound envelopes, a lot of them. He took them out. The first one was dated with the year he was born but about seven months earlier in February. He flipped through the envelopes. They were all dated February in successive years.

He opened the first envelope.

Your mother told me she was pregnant today. I had what I can only describe as a panic attack. I told her I had a vasectomy and hung up on her. I never had a vasectomy. I never got back in touch with your mother either. I was a coward and I'm sorry. I never knew my birth parents. Someone left me on a foster home doorstep when I was a newborn, two days old, apparently. There was a note saying my name and that was it, but there were no Mandevilles in the area and I knew the name was made-up.

So a fake name and no explanation of any kind. I grew up in two different homes in Brewster County, then I aged out. I started a ranch and I put everything I was, everything I had into it. I was always a loner, never got close to anyone. I had girlfriends but would never commit. When I got that call from Annie Dawson, I cried for a good half hour. Sobbed like I hadn't since I was a kid.

That's enough for now.
Yours,
Harlan Mandeville

Gavin sat back, the air gone from his lungs. He opened the next one. Dated a year later. Harlan wrote what he'd done that day, what was on his mind concerning the ranch. He ended it I'm sorry, Harlan Mandeville. There were twenty-eight more just like it. Gavin read every one. Each more impersonal than the last. The last one was dated this year in February. Like the first, it was different from the all the others.

Gavin,
I'm not in good physical shape. My heart is going and the next time I won't survive it. I've been trying to get my affairs in order.

Which has made me think of the past, of course. Everything I've done. I'm sure you've never forgiven me and never will. I've never forgiven myself. I'm sorry for how I treated you all these years. I don't know anything about you. I just know you're my son and I want you to have what was mine. I wish I'd been a different sort of person. Had that been the case, I would have had a son named Gavin.

I'm leaving everything I have to you. Now that it's the end, I can tell you that I wish I had known you. If I can leave you anything besides the Wild Canyon, it's that. I wish I had known you, in every sense of the words. I don't know my birth parents' story, but I

believe in my heart that they would have said
the same to me.
Yours,
Harlan Mandeville

Tears glistened in Gavin's eyes as he read that
last line. And then reread the short letter. In a para-
graph, Harlan Mandeville had left Gavin—and his
own father, if Bill would admit it—a true gift. A
question answered, a hole in his heart filled. With
just one line. I wish I had known you.

When his doorbell rang, this time Gavin hoped
it was Lily. He just wanted to see her, hold her. For
a long time. But standing on the porch in his baggy
jeans and leather vest and a straw hat was Bill
Pearson. Holding a book. The first in the Range
River series. The start of the Adventures of Harlan Mandeville.

Gavin could see Daniel McJones's truck pulling away.

"Daniel said to call him when I'm ready to head
home," Bill said. "But maybe you could drop me
off when I've had my say."

Gavin sucked in a breath. "Sure," he said, opening the door. "Why don't we go sit outside on the
deck? Cup of coffee? Iced tea? Water?"

"I'll take some iced tea if it's sweet," Bill said.

He was looking anywhere but at Gavin, and it made Gavin sure Bill Pearson was in fact his grandfather.

Gavin went into the kitchen and poured two glasses of the sweetened iced tea, handed one to Bill and led the way to the deck, Buddy sunning himself on his bed.

"I call him Buddy, hope that's all right with you," Gavin said. "I named him before I knew you'd called him Arlo."

"Arlo was Harlan Mandeville's dog. Well, one of them. I mean Harlan from these books," he said, holding up the paperback. "Not the flesh and blood man."

Even Buddy was involved in all this, indirectly. Gavin almost smiled at the notion.

There were two padded chairs facing the yard, and Gavin gestured for Bill to sit. The older man set the book and glass on the table between the chairs.

Gavin hung on to his, his throat dry. He took a long sip. He was ready to hear what Bill had to say. And then he'd share what he knew, what he'd read in Harlan's letters.

"I fell madly in love with a girl named Sally when I was seventeen," Bill said. "So pretty. Sweet as can be. She had no family and was hiding from social services till she turned eighteen. My parents didn't approve of her. And when she got pregnant, we kept it secret. We decided we'd run off some-where and have the baby and everything would be okay. And we did run off to Dandelion Falls, small blip on the map two towns over. But she died giving birth, some awful complication, in a free clinic, and I was just turned eighteen and griev-ing and scared. I left the baby on the doorstep of a foster home in that town, with a note saying his name was Harlan Mandeville. I wanted to give him that much—the name of a real hero."

"And then you kept track of him?" Gavin asked, hearing the emotion clog his voice.

"No, I'm ashamed to say I didn't. For a long time. I was all broken up. I couldn't take care of my own son. My girl was gone. I couldn't go home again. So I drifted, took up as a ranch hand and just went from ranch to ranch."

Gavin could imagine that. "How'd you end up at the Wild Canyon, then?"

Bill took a long sip of his drink. "I just hap-pened to see a story in a rodeo magazine about the Wild Canyon and its owner, Harlan Mande-ville. I was shocked. I knew it had to be him. I was already past sixty then, but I got hired as a barn helper because of all my experience, and once I started slowing down too much, they put me as a cafeteria assistant. I lived in one of the cabins with a bunch of young cowboys until I got Daniel out of that flood, and then Harlan thanked me and gave me the old cabin in the woods. For my service to the Wild Canyon." Gavin could see tears shining in the elderly man's eyes.

"But you never told Harlan who you were?" Gavin asked.

Bill shook his head. "I was ashamed. I was scared and alone and just gave him away. It was the hardest thing I'd ever done besides say good-bye to Sally. By the time I found out about the Wild Canyon, he was very successful. I was afraid he'd hate me. Or think I'd come because he was wealthy." Bill hung his head.

"Hang on, Bill. I want to show you something. A letter Harlan left for me. It helped me and I think it'll help you."

"Oh?" Bill asked, tilting his head.

"Buddy," Gavin said, looking at the dog, "keep Bill company for a minute, will you?"

Buddy lifted his head and padded over to Bill's chair, putting his head on Bill's foot.

Gavin smiled, not expecting that. But all sorts of miracles were occurring lately.

He hurried into the house and plucked the last envelope from the bound stack, then went back outside and sat down again. He explained about the accordion file, the first letter, all the others and then the last one.

He handed the letter to Bill.

"'If I can leave you anything besides the Wild Canyon,'" Bill read out loud, "'it's that. I wish I had known you, in every sense of the words. I don't know my birth parents' story, but I believe in my heart that they would have said the same to me.'"

Bill sucked in a breath, his hand flying up to his mouth. "Sally would have. And I wished it every day."

Gavin reached for his hand and Bill held on to it. Buddy edged closer, putting his chin on Bill's thigh.

"You're my grandfather," Gavin said.

Tears shone in Bill's eyes. "I suppose I am."

It took Gavin a few moments to find his voice, to catch his breath, for his heart to slow down. "There are four bedrooms in the main house. I hope you'll consider moving in."

Bill looked at Gavin, then out at the yard, the woods beyond it. "I'm pretty set in my ways. I don't know about moving."

"Well, think about it. I know Buddy-Arlo would be happy to have you close by. And we do have a chance to know each other, Bill. I want us to take that chance."

Bill stood up, tears falling down his cheeks. Gavin stood too and wrapped the elderly man in an embrace.

He could feel something inside him physically shift. His heart expanding, maybe. Making room for Bill Pearson. His grandfather.

And Lily and Micah.

Chapter Sixteen

Lily was nursing Micah when her phone pinged on the table beside her rocking chair. She glanced over at the screen, expecting her mom to be asking if she wanted her to bring over any more of that chocolate lava cake. She definitely did.

But it was a text from Gavin.

Have some news. And something for you.

Lily's heart leaped in her chest. Had he talked to Bill? Was Bill Pearson Harlan's dad? Gavin's grandfather?

She wasn't sure the news was about them. But

if Gavin could get some peace about his past, his family history, she'd be happier. It would help her heart heal. Maybe his would too someday.

Come on over, she texted back. I'm in the nursery.

She'd get up, which she could do with no problem these days, but the little guy in her arms had been fussy today and she wasn't taking the chance that moving would wake him up.

She heard the door open, and then there was Gavin, filling the doorway of the nursery. He looked different, in a way she couldn't put her finger on.

"After we talked earlier," he began, his gaze intense on hers, "when you told me how you felt about me, when I didn't say anything, I was out of my mind, Lily. I loved you from the first day I met you."

"You did not," she said, her voice breaking.

"I did. You came and got me and completely changed my life because of it. Everything you are I got to see that first day by the gate at the Dawson Family Guest Ranch. I followed you to the Wild Canyon because of it. I faced everything I've been running from because of it. Because of you."

Micah stirred and she stroked his wispy hair. If she focused on the baby, she could say the words tripping over one another in her head, in her heart. "But you're leaving."

"I couldn't leave you, Lily. I could try, and I'd probably get all the way to Cheyenne and my next consulting assignment, which I've canceled, by the way, but I would have turned around and come back. I know that now without a doubt."

"How?"

"Because you helped me open my eyes," he said. "You made it so I'd be ready for the truth when it presented itself. And earlier today it did."

"You spoke to Bill?" she asked.

"I did. But before that, I finally opened the accordion folder that Harlan left me." Her eyes widened as he told her about the letters. Thirty of them. "If it hadn't been for you, Lily Gold, I never would have opened the folder. I wouldn't have read those words that got through, that helped me understand. Forgive finally. The old stubborn Gavin would have thrown that folder in the back of a closet, not even curious. But you changed me, Lily. That's how I know that even if I'd left the Wild Canyon, I would have come back for you and Micah. Because I can't live without you. Either of you."

Lily felt her eyes swell with tears. "Well, same here."

"So I'm not too late?" he asked.

"No way," she said.

He smiled. "Good. And it turns out I have a grandfather." He told her about Bill's visit, and Lily found herself crying. "I invited him to move in to the house, but on the way over here, I was thinking that maybe you and Micah could move in with me, and Bill could have your apartment. He'd probably like that."

"As would I," she said.

Gavin got down on one knee and held open the velvet ring box he'd bought from the jeweler in town. "Will you marry me, Lily? I want to spend the rest of my life with you. And I want to be Micah's father."

Lily gasped. "Yes!" she screamed, Micah's eyes half opening, his lip quirking.

Gavin came over and caressed his head, the boy's little eyes closing. He slipped the ring on her left hand.

She stared down at it, almost unable to believe it was sparkling on her finger.

"Can I hold him?" he asked, his gaze on Micah. He slid his hands under the sleeping baby and actually managed to get him into his arms without waking him. He pressed a kiss to Micah's forehead. "I love you so much, Lily. You changed my entire life. I'll spend the rest of mine thanking you."

"Oh, Gavin," she said on a happy sigh. "I love you too. We both love you."

The baby's eyes drifted open halfway, the tiny fist grabbing onto Gavin's pinkie again.

"Told you he wouldn't let you go," she whispered, reaching up to kiss him on his lips.

"I'm home," Gavin said. "With my family."

Lily looked at her engagement ring, then at her bracelet spelling out her son's name, then at her future husband, who held her baby. Their baby.

He'd given her eight weeks. And now they had forever.

Epilogue

All the employees of the Wild Canyon had been invited to Aria and Jonah's wedding. The September evening weather was perfect, high sixties with a light breeze, and a thousand tiny white lights and specially installed light posts illuminated the backyard at the main house.

The bride and groom were very young, both just twenty, but deeply in love, and Gavin had no doubt their love story would be told through generations.

Gavin was the best man, Lily the maid of honor. Bill, who'd moved in to Lily's apartment, was one of the groomsmen, and oh, had the elderly man been touched. *Me?* he'd kept saying to Gavin, his face full of wonder. *They want me to be part of their wedding?* Not long after Bill had told Gavin the story, he'd asked permission to share it with Jonah. Gavin knew the story would help Jonah, change him as it had Gavin. And he'd been right. Now Jonah seemed to regard Bill as an honorary great-grandfather, and the two had developed a special bond.

It's still a sad story, Jonah had said, *but it makes me feel better to know that Harlan did care. He wanted to know you but just couldn't. And he knew it was the same for his birth parents. They both spent all that time, all those decades, on their own, never having real relationships. I'm not gonna be like that.*

He and Aria had been inseparable soon after. Lily had decided to work part-time in the office, bringing Micah with her, and she was training a new assistant since Aria wanted to work at the sanctuary full-time.

The young couple would be part of another wedding party coming on New Year's Day, when Gavin and Lily would take their vows in the gorgeous lodge at the Dawson Family Guest Ranch, where it had all begun. Gavin had filled out the paperwork to adopt Micah. The baby was his in his heart, and soon enough it would be legal.

Almost five months old, Micah had been the

ring bearer at today's ceremony, Gavin helping him out with the proffering of the rings. With the stars twinkling overhead, Gavin had held his baby son in his arms as he and his fiancée watched Aria and Jonah say their "I dos."

He couldn't wait till it was his day, to say his vows, to officially be husband and wife. And their baby son would be there from the beginning.

Heir to their love story.

* * * * *

For more great romances, try these other western stories from Harlequin Special Edition:

Captivated by the Cowgirl
By Brenda Harlen

The Wrangler Rides Again
By Stella Bagwell

Her Wyoming Valentine Wish
By Allison Leigh

Available now wherever Harlequin Special Edition books and ebooks are sold!